THE LAST SHADOW

With an incredible eye for the nuances of New Orleans, America's most interesting city, Michael Allen Zell presents crime fiction with verve, grit, and tenderness. The characters in *The Last Shadow* are people I've known from a distance. Zell's talent allows readers to have access to the hidden dreams and terrors of their lives.

—Maurice Carlos Ruffin, author of *The American Daughters*

Zell demonstrates a gallows humor and a fine ear for entertainment… like the best crime fiction, the story invests deeply in setting, and it succeeds by virtue of its author's palpable love for New Orleans and the people who live there.

—*Los Angeles Review of Books*

What really keeps us turning pages is Zell's authorial voice, his insights into human nature, and the dark sense of humor that comes out of observing city life.

—*The New Orleans Advocate*

THE LAST SHADOW

Michael Allen Zell

MBW
NEW ORLEANS

To Pamela

A LONE FIGURE PEDALED HER BIKE UP ESPLANADE. THERE WERE obvious charms. The narrow grassy neutral ground leading forward like an arrow. The oak trees as watchful sentries stretching to canopy the street. The native sun beaming through and bouncing off of a range of architecture. The cross streets with names like Dorgenois, Crete, and Mystery.

She wasn't feeling the allure, though. Not there to spectate or celebrate. Practicality took precedence, as in, avoiding obstacles. Potholes like baby moon craters. Cars double-parked or veering into the bike lane. Other bicyclists acting erratically. Still, she pedaled on.

Her direction was lakeside. Directions of north, south, east, and west meant nothing on the streets of New Orleans. Not only because of the geographic northwestern tilt by much of the city. The human tilt too. Things were ordinary, different, and differently ordinary in the Crescent City. Soon enough she would reach her destination.

1 THE WAY IS IN THE FORM.

"Doesn't matter what your mind tells you. Your body can do more," said Julius Mosley.

Call it heaven. Call it hell. It's all just as well. Often it feels like too much of New Orleans is broken. Broken people. Broken roads. Too heavy loads. That's the hardest part about the city. When the party inevitably ends, the fortunate continue their haze and unreality in another place. A glitzier one. But others--the born and raised, sinned and saved, rocked and raged--are left with the broken. No Yakamein or Bloody Mary can fix it. Not when the ceiling has been sinking since birth. Getting so low you walk with a hunch. Walls inching in too. That's the thing you can count on. The only old faithful in a temporary world.

"Keep your form right. Solid horse stance," Mosley encouraged. His students made sure feet were pointed forward, spine was straight, and body was loose.

To survive with any measure of balance one must develop a code. A way of life worth living. Or at least recognizing the law of cause and effect. Of course, this makes for an anomaly in a place where alcohol flows through veins and there's easier access to drugs than fresh fruit. Where so many are unafraid to die but terrified to live. Where everyone turns a blind eye to the reality that today's life of the party is tomorrow's discard.

"I like what I see. Root those feet into the ground,"

he added.

Some make it through the wild days intact. Focused. At peace. Secure and unwavering in the knowledge that they are islands in a sea of constant reverie. Sifu Mosley was one of these people.

He had a favorite spot for his class in an area of City Park, steps from Harrison and Marconi. Rain or shine. Hot or cold. Oak trees at least 50-90 years old in that part of the park. Weather was surprisingly pleasant on the fourth Sunday in August. Summer heat and humidity would be back, but it was one of the most beautiful days since April. They were relishing it.

Eight martial arts students were squatting down. Feet apart a bit more than shoulder length. Thighs parallel to the ground. Chins down. Butts tucked in. Each held a light weight or a kettlebell. Mosley walked among the group, only one of them Black like him.

"You wondered why we spent the past six months in deep horse stance. Seemed boring at the time. Your legs are like tree trunks now. Less is more," he called out.

Sifu Mosley smacked both his thighs, checked his watch, and said, "Time! Now here's where it gets fun. Weights to the front, then return to your spot."

The students ranged in age, but like most in this type of fitness, they either grew up liking to fight, were seeking personal growth, or wanted to be like the action stars in Kung Fu movies. Maybe all the above.

It mattered who the teacher was too. It was fitting that "Sifu" was the Chinese word for teacher. Mosley taught a unique style of his own making. It had three parts: 1) Tiger Claw Style or Fu Jow Pai from the legendary 10 Tigers of

Canton. 2) Kali or Eskrima from the Philippines, mainly for the footwork. 3) Tong Bei for the use of distance and Taoist principles. Throw in an honorary 4) To Jeet Kune Do from Bruce Lee for quickly bridging the gap to an opponent and retreating like an American boxer. Add a strong spiritual and philosophical bent too that grounded everything.

Mosley had no name for this. Didn't feel like it was his place as an outsider. A lo fan, foreign devil, teaching Asian culture. He just fit together what made sense to him.

The students stood upright, shook out sore legs, and took their weights to the front. There was a little small talk, respectful chit chat, along the way as they gingerly moved back to their positions. All eyes were on Sifu Mosley.

"Before we start, here's a lil tip," he said. "Keep some change in your pocket. If you get in a situation with an aggressor, throw it to slow them and get away. Works as well as a weapon. Alright, here we go."

He dropped into horse stance, but not as deep as the students had been. In slow motion he alternated punching forward. Left fist striking out, palm down, while in unison his right fist, palm up, pulled back to his waist. Then the opposite. Each time the push and pull worked in unison. But he added a new trick. Left punch with left step in place. Right punch with right step also in place.

Mosley next led with his left foot stepping forward but off to the right side at 3 'o clock while turning his body to continue punching toward the middle. He had an angle on the imaginary opponent he aimed for. Next a right punch and step in place. He repeated the cycle again, staying in the spot, before moving back to his original position.

"Look familiar?" he asked. His students nodded in recognition. They'd wondered why he'd had them practicing footwork that felt like dancing.

He followed that and led with his left foot forward to the left side at a 9 'o clock angle, still turning his body to punch in the middle at an imaginary opponent. His final move after a few steps and strikes on this side was to return once again to his original place.

"You thought all this time I was getting you ready for the club. Now you see. Open triangle or call it open diamond. Messes with your opponent's peripheral and gauging distance. Remember, Kali is footwork with sticks or knife, so you could incorporate that, but what we're doing is taking the best of both worlds. Got it? For centuries, the Filipinos and others were banned from this kind of martial art, so they called it dance in order to practice and continue it."

The students were impressed. Their faces beamed and shone like the first time seeing a chef mixing equal parts flour and oil to make a roux.

Mosley looked at each of them. "Where you begin is where you end. Slow mo first, then strike with power." He paused for effect. "You can do it. Give yourself a little more space," he directed, moving them further apart from each other with his hands before continuing, "For fun, I'll be walking up to each of you with the makiwara board to strike."

"Oh, man," groaned Randy, an anxious bespectacled white man. Like just under 1/3 of New Orleanians and all but one of the students, Randy was a transplant. He originally hailed from Seattle and didn't engage in more-NOLA-than-thou debates with other transplants. It was tempting to chime in with "Fifteen years" when he heard relative newcomers debate the distinction of their five years compared to another's three, but self-restraint and a good sense of humor kept him out of the small fray most of the time.

"It's not a brick," said Mosley. "You'll be fine."

With that Sifu picked up the wooden makiwara board covered with rubber. It was the size of a small bed pillow and had a few cuts into the wood on one end to allow it to give upon being struck. As compared to a tree. A handful of the students looked nervous, a few determined, and one calm. Her name was Maya Gaines. She was the sole born-and-raised student in the group and used to demographics not in her favor in many situations.

Mosley settled them with, "First we breathe deeply. You know how we do it. In--five count--lower belly moves out. Out--five count--belly comes in. Heat it up."

All of them did this together for a few deep breaths.

He guided, "Next drop into horse." They followed.

"Remember, open diamond shape. Step while you strike. Two strikes each fist in the middle, step off to the right while striking in the middle, then back to where you started. Take it to the left, repeat the cycle, and back to where you started again. Got it? Two strikes, each fist, each point. Picture the opponent in the middle you're moving around. Here we go. Slow mo first."

"1," he said as the left punches glided out.

"And," he continued as the right punches followed.

Sifu counted it off, alternating numbers and adding directions of "left," "right," and "back" to move them along. Once they completed the half diamond-half triangle shape, he announced, "Full speed punches."

He kept with the directions while walking among them with the board. The cue of his voice was far more helpful than they'd initially expected. Mosley was savvy enough to hold the board out just before longer arm extension.

Even so, a couple of students shouted out in surprise, three punched softer on the next strike, and Randy fell down. Despite this, Mosley gave each their turn while the group continued making an open triangle with their steps.

Their Tiger Claw strike meets Kali footwork was seen by a group of five young men. They were from rural upstate Louisiana. Bourbon Street was their eventual destination to meet up with other members of the bachelor party, but City Park was close to their house rental. They wanted to be fully in their cups before hitting the French Quarter but had made the illogical decision of drinking Dur beer with ABV barely above lemonade.

Dur, the French term for "tough guy," and its corresponding commercials during NFL football games were what pulled in bros across the US to guzzle swill the French themselves would never sip and only refer to with a sneer as "la pisse." Truth be told, urine itself might have more of a kick than Dur.

Bros from the country were buds.

Bud 1 whispered louder than he realized, "Bud, that's some anime shit."

Bud 2 hollered at the class, "Hey, where's the swords?

Can't be a real ninja without swords."

Led by his guffaws at supposed hilarity, the other buds all laughed in a way that can only be described as ignorant, arrogant, and with more than a hint of menace.

The students didn't know what would happen. Sifu Mosley's back was to the partiers as Maya was next to strike the makiwara board.

Bud 2 felt empowered upon no response. He was the type to elevate the situation if he sniffed perceived weakness from the other.

"Hey, I'm talking to you," he said. "That stuff will get you knocked out in a real fight. Acting all tough but you ain't dick. Especially not the chick."

All five buds snickered at that one. They quickly finished their bottles. Slowly advanced. Stage-whispered among themselves.

Maya was the only woman in the class. Specifically a Black woman and didn't like where all of this was heading. In response to the buds, she paused hesitantly, deferring to Sifu Mosley. He pointed down to say stay put before holding up the makiwara board for her to begin. She took a few deep breaths before starting. Each of her strikes connected firmly. The sound of the board rang out at a level not heard from the others. It popped and echoed, steady and sure.

She had crisp technique, strong resolve, and a fierce fire inside, but she remained mostly calm. Been well-accustomed to the looks and comments of curiosity, desire, or disdain by men since she was barely out of grade school. Since middle school she didn't feel like she was normal after what happened with her parents. Maya began to find her place and peace ever since seeing a martial arts flyer at the coffeeshop back in March and acting on it. The classes brought about an eventual sense of tenacity and purpose that seemed elusive before. Her self-image and confidence were rising too.

Mosley stayed with Maya, keeping the board right in the sweet spot of her strikes. They had such a triumphant song like a drumbeat that even birds in nearby trees took a break from fussing or fornicating to watch from above.

The other students had also stopped the exercise at this point. A few stepped back in anticipation, seeing the growing tension from the slowly advancing buds. Bud 3 smashed his Dur bottle on a tree branch and held the jagged edge out in front of him.

At this, Mosley faced the partiers, and without a word took a few steps to flank Maya. Again, she waited, out of respect for him, but each sensed what they needed to do.

Both Sifu and Maya began to punch-and-step forming the open diamond shape, but after the movements on the left side Mosley stepped strongly forward and to the middle two steps to make a new shape. Maya wasn't ready for that move, but she quickly adjusted and did the same. They both then shifted back to the right to complete the diamond shape. After a few of these full diamond strike and step shapes, they had the keen attention of the buds.

"We're here in peace," said an unwavering Sifu Mosley, who then clicked his tongue to signal that Maya follow his lead. The two of them stayed in place but continued striking. 1-2, 1-2.

The alpha-bud who had first whispered about the class said to his friends, "Look, let's keep it moving. They don't want this smoke. Alright, bud."

This was the preferred out. They didn't want to fight. Only to intimidate.

Bud 2 parted with "We were just fuckin' with you. Come on, bud."

With that all five buds staggered away.

Maya moved her arms so that her hands crossed in the middle of her chest like an X, swept them out like grand wings to make an arc above her, before palms came back to meet and press together up high. She then dropped them to just below eye level in prayer position. Her joined fingertips pointed at the sky while she bowed slightly.

Both Maya and Mosley paused for a moment, stunned. "Who are you?" wondered Mosley, though he didn't speak it. Maya was thinking the same thing about herself.

Mosley nodded in respect and encouragement. Saying in his mind, "Proud of my people. She was the only one in class who could've done this."

"I see you, sister. Next time, don't hesitate. Follow your instinct. What's inside you will lead you," is what he finally spoke aloud.

If Maya was one to smile, this would've been the time. Unfortunately, she'd had little to smile about for so long that she'd fallen out of practice, so instead she briefly made eye contact before pointing upward.

Mosley saw the tree he knew well. Branches either curving or bent at 90 degree angles inward to City Park. Likely from hurricanes over the years.

"Right. Bend or you break," he finally said.

Another group passing through the oaks came upon

the class. A mama duck and seven ducklings in line behind her. They were on their way from one bayou to another. Seeing them made both Sifu Mosley and Maya feel that all was well with the world.

2 PATIENCE LEADS TO GREAT VIRTUE.

Julius Mosley was reeling from what had happened. The students closed out the class by making right fists and pushing them firmly up against angled left palms as they bowed slightly. He did the same and chatted a bit while they gathered themselves, cleaned up the broken glass, and walked to their cars. Except Maya, who got around by bicycle and hurried off.

Sifu was struck by the calm steady will of his star student. It was inspiring. Made him want to be a better teacher. This was lifting him as he started up the car and called his wife Samira shortly after.

He started with, "I'm heading home, my love. You should have seen it today."

"Really? What happened?" she asked.

Mosley enthused, "I thought Maya was good, but man, the way she followed my lead. The mindset too. What this is all about. In the real world."

Samira wondered, "She's your only Black student, right?"

"At this point."

"You know how it is. We excel if given half a chance. For real. Not when they talk that jibber jabber but still do anything to keep their own shine."

Mosley blew out air through his teeth. "This ain't that. You know how I do."

"I know, baby. Maya sounds like she's a quick learner

and just needs her talent nurtured. You're the person for it too."

"That's exactly it," he agreed. "She's got ice in her veins. I'm envious."

Samira teased, "The student becomes the teacher. You think it took you a while longer?" She knew the answer.

"Look, it took me 30 years. Some of us have a steep learning curve. The guys in the 7th precinct didn't call me Moto because I kept my mouth shut. And yes, the teacher can definitely learn from the student."

She laughed. It wasn't new information, but the difference between that person and the man she was talking to was startling.

He continued, "If you'd known me then. Walking mess. Falling down drunk."

"I can barely picture it," she said sweetly. "Baby, would you swing by the pharmacy on the way home. My prescription's in."

"Sure, I'll pick it up for you," he said. "The one by St. Charles and Felicity?"

"Mmm hmm."

"Alright," he said. "A lil Sunday drive."

"I'm surprised you remember what day of the week it is," she teased.

Mosley laughed. "Living off that pension. Every day's the weekend."

Samira returned his laugh with her own.

"Okay, baby," he said. "See you soon."

"Be safe."

"You got it," he replied.

Mosley wasn't aware that the second line that

Sunday was in his neck of the woods. It was the first one after summer break. In season, they alternated between Uptown, mostly Central City, and further downriver. It was wise to be up on which part of town it was rolling in.

Unfortunately, Julius Mosley got caught by virtue of taking his usual route through Central City, turning onto Magnolia to pick up a plate at Heard Dat on the way, and realizing too late that he wouldn't be continuing on very soon. Backing up wasn't an option at that point as the advancing crowd swelled around him. He turned off the car, sat on the hood, and watched the dancers stepping and strutting to brass band music. Though it was the Valley of Silent Men Social Aid & Pleasure Club, there was nothing silent about it.

He called Samira back too.

"It's gonna be a minute. I think you can hear why."

3 VITALITY COMES FROM CONTINUING.

Maya Gaines was biking back on Esplanade from City Park to one of her restaurant jobs in the French Quarter. She had her phone on speaker mode.

"Hi Auntie. Brassy called me in early. I'm going straight there. Extra hours."

Aunt Nekisha Fisher replied, "Stacking that money, my baby."

"Stacking pennies maybe," said Maya ruefully.

"I know Maya, but you've been blessed. God will continue to bless you. About to be a female Bruce Lee too. I'm so proud of how you threw yourself into a new situation head-on."

"Yes, Aunt Kish," Maya said.

She paused and craned her neck. Coming her way on the other side of the neutral ground was a police escort heading up a small group that was barely swinging their arms to the music by the brass band leading them. Hips wouldn't be moving until later that night. The wedding party trudged, but loudly so, wanting to make sure everyone within earshot had no doubt they were having the time of their lives.

"Now, look," Aunt Nekisha continued, "Stay clear of that second line, hear? Too many knuckleheads trying to catch somebody lacking. I don't want you in the middle of a shootout."

Maya said, "It's a tourist group. No dancing at this

one. Can't even buy a plate."

"Still, you be safe. Don't need no plate anyway. Brassy good food. Call me when you're heading out after your shift. Love you."

"Yes, Aunt Kish. Love you too," said Maya.

She continued on, passing the wedding group heading toward City Park, and wouldn't have to deal with her own crowd issue for several blocks. Trying to get through merrymakers kicking it up along the streets of the French Quarter. She was accustomed to it all, but that didn't mean she liked it. At a certain point it was just easier to walk her bike into the Bourbon Street masses for a half block until she reached Brassy restaurant not far from Canal Street.

4 A FIXED MIND KNOWS NO OTHER.

"Jimmy, Jimmy, Jimmy. Repeat what he said."

The man sitting behind the desk in the back office of the New Orleans East jewelry store had two first names. This was fitting. He also had two personalities and faces depending on who he was with. One was seemingly friendly and benevolent. To be fair, that side of him did exist, though it was scant compared to his prevailing personality.

Vinh Nguyen was the upstanding citizen. Vinnie was the ruthless criminal. The tell in any situation was his eyes. Some things cannot be finessed. No matter how much practice. No matter how hard he tried to add a twinkle or lighter touch to his gaze, the orbs were shorthand to his life. Neither their microscope nor telescope was pretty. He had committed unspeakable acts. Soulless ones. Mainly against his own Vietnamese people and others of Asian descent.

He was glaring at two of his men, Jimmy and Cuong, who were seated across from the desk. Jimmy was holding a blood-soaked handkerchief over his nose. Nguyen was rubbing his bruised knuckles and shaking his head.

Cuong leaned forward to speak, but he received a prompt signal to stop. Nguyen pointed at Jimmy. Shook his twitching finger a few times.

"From him."

Jimmy swallowed once and a second time before he

spoke.

"*Đại ca*, boss, with all respect. I'm only repeating what they said."

Nguyen's volume was measured. "Say the words again."

Jimmy deflected. "I don't think such a thing myself."

The elder man stood up and spoke louder.

"Be a man and say it."

The deep breath Jimmy took made his broken nose hurt more.

"But when I said it before you…"

Nguyen struck his desk. Though he used the side of his right fist, the impact carried to his sore knuckles, which made him angrier.

"Say it, you useless fucking asshole!" he thundered in full Vinnie mode.

Cuong winced. Jimmy sunk into his chair as he blurted it out.

"Bao Vu said…" He paused and closed his eyes. "Said you were weak. Called you a rice farmer."

With that, Nguyen swung both arms to clear off everything from his desk, all except the security camera and the bottle of wine with the dead cobra inside. Vinnie and Cuong were glad that the items on the floor weren't going to be used as projectiles. On the other hand, Nguyen was growing more heated. His pupils dilated and pulsated like steel strobes.

"When your nose heals, I'm gonna break it again. I've worked too hard for too long to have a skinny little bitch like Bao Vu try to get a piece of my business."

He appeared to be hurt inside.

"And my own man lets it stand."

Cuong tried again. "*Đại ca*, boss, I could see from the car. Jimmy was outnumbered eight-to-one."

This was not the way to calm the boss, but Cuong had nothing else. He knew it before, during, and after Nguyen shook his head in disbelief and looked to the sky.

"I was once side-by-side with Teardrop and Little Cobra," said Nguyen. "Now I'm looking at Useless Mouse and Fucking Fuck. *Máu lồn* and *máu lồn*. Shitty person times two."

He took a deep breath, sat down, and reflected. Jimmy and Cuong dared not interrupt him.

"Bao Vu will pay," Nguyen finally said. "I will save face and he will pay for this. He will drown in a rice field, in fact. He is a young man who will not become old."

The two men nodded vigorously in agreement.

Nguyen continued. "If our people use a drug, it will come from me. Only me. If they fuck a *đĩ*, a prostitute. If they buy a fake Rolex. If they pay for protection. If they bet on roosters fighting. You hear me? If they fucking blink. It comes from only me. Hear that?"

Jimmy and Cuong swung their heads more affirmatively than before.

"He owns no real estate, so I can't hit him there. At least that I know of. It doesn't matter anyway."

Nguyen lowered his head.

"I don't have an enforcer. Didn't need one before. I need a man who will stand strong if eight-to-one odds."

He glared at them.

"Handle the whole room. An enforcer. How can we call ourselves Ghost Dragons without it?"

He pulled up his right sleeve and jabbed his left index finger at the inked letters "GD."

At risk of his situation becoming quickly worse, Jimmy volunteered a useful nugget a little too eagerly.

"*Đại ca*, boss, I heard that Bao Vu was trying to work drugs with the Blacks in the 7th ward."

This caught Nguyen by surprise, who thought, looked at Jimmy with disbelief, and then reeled with this new knowledge. Jimmy nodded in confirmation.

"I don't know if I'm more surprised he would do business with *mi dang*, Black people, or that you didn't lead with that to keep from a broken nose. I have a building there. Restaurant our people run. The answer is there. Someone will know about Bao Vu's plans. Maybe where he lays his head. He will pay. A farmer, eh? Jimmy, go have a doctor fix your nose. Cuong, get the car ready. I need to step up front for a moment."

Jimmy winced at the nose pain while getting up and walking, as he and Cuong hurried out the back as quickly as they could without showing their rush.

Nguyen straightened his clothing, then opened the main door into the jewelry store. A handful of customers were shopping. He worked his way through them. Smiling warmly. Shaking hands. Bowing slightly. Turning on Vinh-charisma.

"*Xin chào*. Hello everyone. I am Vinh Nguyen. Welcome to my store. You picked the perfect time. Thank you for coming."

He next directed a pronouncement heard 100s of times before by the three clerks on the other side of the glass showcase counter.

"The best deals for them. Make sure."

He said it and he meant it. This was who Vinh Nguyen was.

Nguyen shook a few more hands by using both of his and bowing slightly on the way out the front door to where Cuong had his car ready.

5 QUESTIONS REVEAL SPIRIT.

The man sitting at the table way Uptown in the Riverbend dining room was known by one first name. It was different in the past, but a particular event in his life was the catalyst. The beginning of change. Shedding skin. Transformation. The former side of him did exist, for it was part of him too, but years of habits and focus had made the younger him unrecognizable.

Decor in the dining room and the rest of the bungalow was minimalist. Simple but tasteful. An about face from the rat race. If the rectangular table was a compass, then Julius Mosley was facing East, his wife Samira looked toward the West, son A.J. to the North, and daughter Flora to the South. College break was about to finish up for the young Mosley's, and their parents were already anticipating it.

Most called the man at the head of the table Mosley or Mos, but this was family.

"This is what it's all about. People spend their lives searching, but family and peace are it. The sun and moon inside us," said Mosley.

"Yes daddy," dashed out Flora in a heard-it-all tone.

Samira tilted her head to the right at her daughter, paused, and turned back to her husband.

"She's young. She'll come around."

Flora fussed, "What's that mean?" A.J.'s lips had been pursed in bemused relief that focus wasn't on him.

He couldn't resist chiming in, though.

"It means you're ungrateful."

"A.J., stop," responded Samira.

He shrugged at his mother before smirking at his sister. The focus was on him, so he decided to have fun with it and sniffed hard.

Flora glared so strongly at him that her eyebrows quickly sunk from their high arches like a mountainous terrain crumbling to the ground and forming two valleys.

Julius Mosley narrowed his own eyes at A.J. "You have a cold in the summer?"

"It's his allergies," said Flora a little too quickly.

A.J. was enjoying himself. "Mmm hmm," he said. "My allergies."

At an attempt to clear the air and update the family, Samira changed the subject.

"O-kay, there's a storm about to enter the Gulf of Mexico. Let's check our hurricane prep tonight."

"Definitely," agreed Mosley, who wasn't switching from the subject-at-hand quite yet.

"What are you up to?" he asked to his left and right.

A.J. reassured. "Nothing, dad. What were you like in New York in your 20s?"

"What do you mean? I was a young man trying to figure out the world and my place in it."

Flora was biting her lip and locking discouraging eyes with her brother. She projected her thoughts at him to let it go.

Though A.J. acted like he didn't see her, it gave him ammunition to continue.

"I mean, did you party a lot? Act wild?"

Mosley was curious at the questioning and getting a little irritated.

"Like everyone, I made mistakes," he said. "Had a lot of growing up to do. Why all this?"

A.J. like a butterfly flitting along, "No reason. Did you do drugs?"

Mosley and Samira exchanged glances before both looked at their kids.

"Hold up. Are you two doing drugs?" Julius Mosley demanded.

"No, no," was the mutual response with hands invested in articulating it as much as words.

Mosley paused to calm himself, breathed in deeply through his nose, and held it for a few seconds, before expelling the air back out. He was so well-versed in this he did it without a sound. Samira was steaming but waited on him to begin once he raised a finger in her direction to say, "I'll go first."

"Look, New Orleans right now. Last week, two women firing shots out of their car on I-10. Not at anybody. Just because they can."

"What's that got to do with drugs?" asked A.J.

A younger version of Mosley would have rattled his son's cage, but the sage veteran just said "Fix your face when you talk to me," and stared his son down until A.J. looked away.

Samira's tone didn't betray her frustration. She wanted to inform, not frighten.

"It's the state of the city. They only got caught because of their video bragging about it on social media. Today the judge said house arrest and gave them a slap on the wrist. After they turned themselves in. Said there was no proof it was really them."

Mosley seconded, "After they turned themselves in. See. Your mother follows the news. She knows."

Flora's folly was to feel emboldened. But deflection felt good to her.

"You didn't answer A.J.'s question. This sounds like do as I say, not as I did."

"Really? That's what you're hearing," snapped Samira.

A rare flash of anger showed in Julius Mosley.

"New Orleans is too wild right now to stumble around like a wasted idiot and think it's Disney World. Get your minds right. Both of you. We're gonna talk about this later," he said.

"Yes, daddy. A.J.'s being a weirdo," said Flora.

At that, the table got quiet as Julius and Samira Mosley exchanged glances.

6 SOME PEOPLE FLOW DOWNWARDS.

Brassy was a New Orleans restaurant perfectly situated and geared to its target audience on the upper end of Bourbon Street. Close to the hotels? Check. Name that sounded both like a jazz instrument as well as meaning showy and loud? Check. Menu a mix of local standards such as Crawfish Etoufee and Red Beans & Rice along with a mish mosh of pasta, burgers, and platters? All of them Creole Cajuned and Cajun Creoled to within an inch of their American bar food life? Check. Although tonight they were pushing the Brassy Steak, which wasn't half bad.

The restaurant, like many, wasn't so much about the food anyway, since that would only get you a hair above breaking even. The alcohol needed to flow for the money to grow. The visitors were happy to oblige. Some thought that the infamous street was named after the whiskey. In reality, it received its moniker care of the French royal family in the early 1700s. One would barely need to step outside and walk far from Brassy's front door to see the numerous signs the street should be now named after—Big Ass Beers!

Not only Bourbon. Dauphine should be called Don't Let 'Em Catch You Without A Weapon at 2 a.m. Street due to muggers waiting for drunks. Decatur should be renamed Daytime Tourist T-shirts & Daquiris Street and Royal dubbed Daytime Tourists with Moolah, But Look

Out For Fake Antiques Street.

As was typical, regardless of any New Orleans street, the front of the house staff at Brassy were majority white while the back of the house were majority people of color. The latter included Chef Earl Armstead, who had worked himself up from dishwasher two decades ago. The unambitious recipes were not his doing but those of the owner who came from a long line of restaurateurs and scoundrels. Giving the people what they want had worked for decades. If they didn't like it, there'd be plenty more to fill the tables tomorrow. And the next day.

If it was up to Chef Earl, he'd cook up his version of Granny Augusta's stewed chicken, mac 'n cheese, and seafood-stuffed baked potato. But while food that originally came from the 9th ward back by the Florida Canal might be manna from heaven for some, it wouldn't make it anywhere near the Brassy menu. He had a private dream, though even he didn't expect that a scant three years later, his own restaurant, 9th Ward Assassin, would first come to life by Chef and team cooking outside a bar on Claiborne.

In the meantime, Brassy it was. Among the group in the kitchen was Maya Gaines. She worked as a Prep Cook. It was a busy Sunday night, and Maya was chopping vegetables and slicing meat. Elvin, who was there for the summer, was doing the same along with salads, as necessary.

Chef Earl checked a new ticket and called out, "Eight-top with steak. That's seventeen all day."

Various responses rung out. "Eight more. Seventeen all day." "Don't hate on eight." "Give me a dime, I only got eight."

Maya hadn't noticed any reaction from Elvin, so she said quietly, "That's eight more salads, E."

He nodded. Made no eye contact. Said, "Mmm hmm. Heard that."

She continued to keep her voice down both for the eye-in-the-sky recording everything and also not knowing who in the vicinity could be trusted.

"You just know it's Shaun's table. He's on a double. Moody anyway. Gets another 1-star review again, he blame it on slow salads."

This got Elvin worked up. "Shaun kiss my ass."

As if beckoned, a stressed out, clean cut, hands moving, nice-for-what type young white man stepped big into the kitchen as if it was his own.

"Alright, people. Let's pick it up," he clapped.

Chef Earl had been there before. He pointed at himself.

"To me. I'm your P.O.C."

Shaun barely looked in his direction as he continued to the entire kitchen.

"Point-of-contact, yes, but I just added a steak eight-top to point-of-sale. Everybody back here needs to make it happen."

He faced mostly blank annoyed faces, aimless nods, or the backs of those who all of a sudden needed to turn and take care of something important.

But not Elvin.

"Yessir. 'Back here' making it happen all day," Elvin said professionally, but with more than a hint of sarcasm.

Shaun's pregnant pause held so long its water broke

while he studied Elvin.

"Good," he finally spat out and spun on his heels to leave the kitchen. Several made obscene gestures or shook their heads.

Chef Earl was fuming but took a deep breath and called out, "Alright, alright," to calm his crew. "Get out your feelings and handle this shit," he added.

Elvin was hissing like oil dripping on a hot skillet.

"Point-of-sale P.O.S. Piece-a-shit. I got your 'back here.'"

"Don't pull me into your mess. I need this job," said Maya.

Elvin had something for her too.

"Right, right. Little Miss above it all. It happens because we let it happen."

Maya paused.

"Don't play with me," she said.

"I'll be back in college soon while you're still here. Cuz I'm building," Elgin scoffed. "Probably end up buying a place like this. Act right and maybe I hire you."

Maya was about to respond to him but thought better of it. His words stung. He didn't know she'd left LSU. Definitely didn't know why. Maya wasn't about to tell him either. She turned her lips inside her mouth and closed it firmly, same as she'd done since childhood to make sure not a single word could slip out.

Elgin expected her to come at him, but when she didn't and went back to her work, he muttered "No lip having ass," because that was his way.

Meanwhile Shaun was pouring bottles of Malbec for the table of eight. They had driven over from Florida as

they did every year for their annual family get together in
New Orleans.

7 LIFE IS SIMPLE, DO FOR OTHERS, AND TAKE TIME TO BREATH.

WHILE NIGHTLIFE IN NEW ORLEANS WAS BEGINNING TO AWAKEN and hum, Julius Mosley was sitting still. At least his physical body was. His mind was active. Meditation to him wasn't about trying to be empty of thoughts but rather the ancient Buddhist concept of tonglen. When breathing in, he would also consciously take in the pain and suffering of others. When breathing out, he would send out joy and happiness to the world.

Though his eyes focused downward, he could see various plants, including the bonsai trees he'd so carefully shaped and wired into place. Though his deep breathing was concentrated in and out through his nose, he could smell the candle and incense lit earlier. Though his body was still, he couldn't help but recall the physicality of the various martial arts weapons and items around. Though his ears were turned inward, the flow of water in his fountain stilled him by its movement. And though his mind was seesawing with the ebb and flow of joy and pain, he never forgot his family inside the house.

Next to the candle was a small hardcover book covered with black cloth. It was his peace and oracle, his wisdom and wonder, the words that served his soul to awaken his formerly unconscious mind. Its title in red letters was *The Last Shadow* and its author unknown. Mosley had randomly come across it at a time he was in need. This same worn book had been with him over two decades. It had 39 entries. Each with a drawing on the opposite page. Sometimes he would flip to a random page. Other days he would start at the beginning. Today he chose the random flip.

The book was held open with a small stone placed on the right side to hold the latter pages and a second larger stone on the left side to hold the previous pages. The verso side showed a drawing of the woods. The recto side had the following entry: "Life is simple, do for others, and take time to breath."

Mosley rose up, shook out his legs, and slowly went through a Tai chi sequence.

While he worked through this, A.J. and Flora were arguing in her room over the subject of conversation at dinner. Samira was organizing hurricane items such as canned food, water, batteries, and flashlights.

A.J. and Flora continued fussing at each other on their way out the front door while Mosley dropped into horse stance and went through the full diamond shape of strikes and steps he and Maya had done earlier. Since she was at a stopping point, Samira joined him outside.

On the right corner, "What's going on with the kids?"

"I don't know, but I don't like it," said Samira.

On the middle back, "When I finish here, it's time to talk."

"They both just left," Samira offered.

On the left corner, "To go where?"

Samira was skeptical. "The usual friends, or at least that's what they said."

On the middle top, "Hmm. I don't like it either. Tiger

time."

While Mosley shaped his hands into tiger claws and stretched his wrists to loosen up the tendons, Samira walked over with a 20-pound sandbag. She started with a light underhand toss that he caught with his right claw. Next, he tossed it up about half a foot before catching it on its way down with his left claw. Back and forth. Palms faced down the whole time.

Samira sat nearby, feeling the breeze and the ambiance, so she called out, "Ready for the levee?"

He nodded, put the sandbag down, and traded it for ten iron rings. The two of them walked alongside the house until they hit the street and continued on for a ½ block. Across the train tracks and up the earthen levee until they reached the top. The river was low since rain had been light that summer.

When each of Mosley's wrists were looped with an equal number of rings, which added almost eight pounds per side, he dropped into deep horse stance. Alternating between arms extended forward, palms pushing together as if in prayer, and palms pushing each left and right side as far as his arms could extend was enough to finish his night. The rings barely rung, so steady his balance held while transitioning through each new position.

Samira sat, taking in the evening sky and the chop of the water.

8 STORM CLOUDS ARE LORDS OF THE SKY.

Vinh Nguyen rubbed his stomach and announced to Cuong, "We will get our bellies filled. Then time for answers."

Cuong had his antenna up.

"Yes *đại ca*, boss. But I feel like…"

This was a word to set off Nguyen.

"Feel? I don't pay you to feel. You kidding me? Back in the day…"

He collected himself and took a bite.

Outsiders and even born-and-raised locals often have a limited-lens view of New Orleans history and culture. Back in colonial days, the French ran things for around 45 years, but the Spanish did so for only a few years less. The prevailing look of the French Quarter comes from the latter. Though most would know the scourge of slavery brought a population from western Africa, fewer might realize that the aftermath of the Haitian revolution tripled the free-person-of-color number in New Orleans and greatly led to the Afro-Caribbean feel of the city known to this day.

Also, the Germans introduced farming, so less reliance on provision ships. The Cajuns came down from Canada but headed off to the rural areas quickly enough. Add to that the Irish, Italians from Sicily, Latin Americans largely from Honduras, and all the other ethnic groups from around the world coming through a port city. This is not to discount the undersung influence by the indigenous people who saw the benefit of trading areas well before the French came along.

More recently, after the Vietnam War, the prevailing Asian population in New Orleans came largely in the late 1970s. From fishing to nail salons, from growing food to running corner stores, the Vietnamese population is integral in the city. There are about 10,000 in the New Orleans area, largely in what is officially Village de L'Est but called Versailles, at the far edge of the city. Around half of that number live across the river on the West Bank.

A Vietnamese-run restaurant in the majority Black 7th ward was not out of the ordinary. That was where they'd been allowed in. It was entirely natural to have Fried rice and po boys, Pho and white beans, spicy boiled crawfish and turkey necks. Plus a few standard grocery and drugstore items. This was the case at Southern Seafood in the long ramshackle building on Saint Bernard.

Vinh Nguyen and Cuong were seated in the back with both chairs angled to face the front door. Theirs was one of the few tables, as this was mostly a to-go place. The wait staff made sure all was well for one reason. Nguyen was the owner. Otherwise, their relationship with patrons, and vice versa, was edgy at best.

Nguyen cared little about any of that. He was content to slurp his noodle soup with dumplings.

"Back in the day I shared an apartment with seven other guys. All of us young and crazy. First floor of the building was a dumpling place. Just to get outta that apartment I'd eat my noodle and dumpling soup in the restaurant. Or the park…" His sentence tailed off, "across the street."

He paused and stared off in the distance before continuing.

"Chives and pork dumplings every time. Made from scratch. That's why I have it on the menu here. Because back in the day doesn't need to stay there. Can be here now too. Ghost Dragons were feared back then. That can be again. Don't tell me what you fucking feel. That's useless. Tell me how we can make it happen."

Cuong looked sheepish and chagrined as if he'd just been seen eating shrimp off the floor. Luckily he was rescued by Sister Pat coming to the table. She managed the restaurant and was no nonsense.

"Hi Vinnie. How's things, you fucking fuck?" she said in a way very few could. Her manner was typically stone cold, but this greeting allowed for merriment.

Nguyen needed that and he laughed deeply.

"My friend, so good to see you. You look great, Sister Pat."

She laughed in turn.

"You talk with your *cặc*, cock, but he must be blind. What brings you to this part of town beyond dumplings and noodles? It's good, right? Dumplings made fresh the way you like."

"Very good," he praised. "Compliments to the kitchen."

Nguyen leaned toward her and lowered his voice.

"You get mostly *mi dang*, Black people, in here. Have you heard anything about Bao Vu making business moves with them?

Sister Pat looked at him quizzically. If the question hadn't come from Vinh Nguyen himself, she would have assumed the question asker to be stupid and quickly let them know it.

"They don't trust us. We definitely don't trust them. But Bao Vu is foolhardy. It's news to me what you wonder. But I know who to ask. One of the upstairs regulars. Hold on a moment,"

She walked to the cash register, opened it, and rummaged through a stack of receipts. Once she found the one she was looking for, she took it back to the table.

"This is him," she said. "Kiri Price. They call him Tree. Very tall. Every day, same thing. Two-piece fried chicken. Fried rice. Coca-Cola. He is…let me think… Apartment 4 upstairs. Not his lucky day."

Cuong felt comfortable enough to speak.

"Never his lucky day with that number. I'll get what you need *đại ca*, boss."

He straightened up and checked his gun, ready to show his worth.

Vinh gestured with his open palm up to say, "Go do it." As Cuong left the restaurant, Nguyen and Sister Pat continued their conversation.

Cuong stepped outside and walked along the front of the neglected building. Passed the "No Loitering" sign posted above two men leaning against the wall. Made sure they saw him clearly hold the gun in his waistband so they wouldn't follow. He wasn't surprised the iron security door was ajar. After a few steps in, he walked rotted wood stairs to the 2nd floor. The fact it was wide open and anyone could get in right off the street, especially near a busy intersection, told him everything he needed to know.

He strode with confidence up and across the balcony to Apartment 4, cleared his throat, and knocked.

Cuong tucked the gun in his back waistband so that both hands were free and he appeared unarmed. Put arms out in front of him to give the appearance that he posed no danger.

"Rent reduction," he called out.

After a pause, a voice from inside responded.

"Who this?"

"I'm here to reduce your rent," Cuong persisted.

"Fuck you say? For real? Ain't due for two weeks."

Cuong added extra earnestness and a cliched Asian emphasis to his voice.

"Yes, sir. Save you big money."

The door quickly opened. A man who only cleared the doorway by a couple of inches pointed his gun down at Cuong.

"You think I'm stupid. Rent reduction. It never goes down. You play, you pay. Give me that watch."

He gestured for Cuong to enter with his free hand.

"C'mon, run it. Wallet too. Get your ass in here."

As soon as the door closed, there was brief commotion but no gunshots or voices. Only a few sharp thuds that fit in perfectly with the sounds of the street.

Downstairs in the restaurant, Vinh Nguyen praised Sister Pat.

"*Cục vàng*, special person you are. We have many years, my sister."

She nodded in agreement.

"Who would have thought, Vinnie," she said. Same

refugee camp in the Philippines after our families fled Vietnam. Now here after all these years. Okie dokie. Piss off this nostalgia."

Nguyen continued his riff Cuong had heard earlier.

"Piss it all off, but back in the day matters. I remember my family escaping in a fishing boat. You do too. I wasn't even ten yet. When we finally get to this country, what's waiting? Winter."

Sister Pat wrapped her arms around herself and shook as if shivering.

"Oh, my. Makes my bones cold thinking about it," she said.

Nguyen nodded, tightening his mouth and eyes.

"Made us tougher," he said. "Who else could do what we did? Our people. Always have. Always will. Did what we needed to do."

"Speaking of," she said and pointed above them. "I wonder how it's going upstairs."

If she and Nguyen were to have followed Cuong's path and opened the apartment door, they would have seen him holding his own gun in his right hand and Tree's in his left. Both were trained on an angry and antsy, bruised and bloody Kiri Price sitting on his couch. The window behind him showed no more than a back view of the billboard outside. Cuong was there for information on Bao Vu at the behest of his boss. He was quickly finding out that was only the beginning of what he could accomplish with Tree. Cuong felt like the cat that ate the bird.

People often talk about "the game" in reverence, probably from watching too many movies. Maybe from longing for a time since past. Whatever the reason, reality was different. Despite what many swore so strongly about snitching you would think it was inked on their foreheads, in actuality there were far more CI's than realized. Confidential Informants dropping dimes.

Once arrested, the vast majority talk. Loyalty is a soldier who isn't behind bars, doesn't want to be, or is A1 until a better deal comes along. Long term thinking doesn't exist. What can you get right here, right now? And that included Tree.

9 RAISE NOT VOICE, HAND, OR WEAPON IN ANGER.

IT WAS CLOSE TO MIDNIGHT WHEN MAYA CLOCKED OUT AT Brassy, collected her bike, and called it a night. The wall of people on Bourbon Street made it impossible to navigate. Didn't matter it was Sunday night. Her route was to get down to Chartres, closer to the river, and take that one-way across the French Quarter. She would continue past Esplanade for just the hint of Frenchmen Street, where the party was also going, before making only her second left turn. At that point it was a straight shot all the way up Elysian Fields.

Maya was exhausted and vibing to music to pass the time. Ambient and drifting, anchored by beats. More chill, less street.

It wasn't a carefree ride. Being conscious of potholes, reckless drivers, tipsy pedestrians, and anything unexpected came with the territory. The mindset to have was wisdom, not knowledge.

Knowledge was recognizing stop signs. Wisdom was pausing before biking across the intersection in case a driver or another bicyclist barreled toward her, disregarding their stop sign. Knowledge was the simple distinction of the Elysian Fields car lanes being separate from the bike lanes. Wisdom was to be prepared for a drunk or inattentive driver veering into her lane, or even other bicyclists pedaling in her direction, which would force one of them to scoot into the adjacent car lane. Expect the unexpected might be the only steady mantra in New Orleans.

There was no way, of course, for her to anticipate items in the roadway, especially at night. Whether called caltrops, ninja throwing spikes, or makibishi, small sharp objects have been used for centuries. Mostly in times of war to slow pursuers. In the past 25 years by U.S. law enforcement in the form of spike strips that stretched across the entire road to end a chase. None of these deflated her front tire, however.

In actuality, this was the source--the house on the corner of Elysian Fields and Burgundy had needed a new roof for decades. The damage from Hurricane Ida last year on the anniversary of Hurricane Katrina made it a priority. Though the roofers had used a dumpster and a magnetic nail sweeper when they were done in mid-November, nails had bounced across the side street next to an empty lot. There they sat in gutter hibernation for months, covered by leaves, until little by little, wind and the impact from traffic slowly moved the old round-head inch-long nails to bridge the twelve feet gap closer to the main intersection.

One of the five squirmed into the street just after dusk that night, where it flattened the left front tire of teenage thieves ready for action. This knocked the daily total of car thefts down from the average of 19 to 15. Steady writhing took the second nail further into the street an hour later where it promptly punctured the right rear tire of a chef on her way to do an evening pop-up event. By running late and staying later than expected, she had the luck to meet an investor with deep pockets who thought her vision for cupcakes and cookies with unique images and phrases would be a hit on a bigger scale.

The remaining three roofing nails inched their way throughout the evening closer and closer to the bike lane. Those who traversed it had no idea what might have been for them. By the time Maya Gaines dodged a handful of tourists walking out in front of her when she crossed Frenchmen Street, the nail trio was in place. Had the bartender bicyclist two blocks in front of her on Elysian Fields not been texting, which briefly edged him into the car lane, Maya would've been biking past a person with flat tires instead of her. But instead it was Maya who ended up with two nails in her front tire and one in the back, rendering her bike instantly unusable.

"Uhhhhh, so tired of this," she said, checking that her headband was still on straight and pocketing the three nails. Maya would be walking her bike the remaining distance. It was the only way. Aunt Nekisha had answered her call when leaving Brassy, but she was still at work.

Maya was frustrated but not surprised. It was the third time she had to walk her bike home from work for the same reason this year. After moving over to the sidewalk, she continued up Elysian Fields.

Over the next seven blocks, she couldn't help but see that there were no fewer than three new road work projects on side streets. This came as less surprise than the nails on the street.

If there was a plot, a citywide conspiracy, to aggravate as many citizens as possible, it would succeed no better than the City of New Orleans' road work plan. Block after block all over the city had been torn up, in some cases with full-on excavation, but the work had stopped for several months after that. There were lakes in streets, and unused human-sized piles of dirt that had sprouted vegetation. In perhaps the most perverse twist, in some cases one half of the street was torn up and eventually repaved while the other side sat unpaved. It was complete disarray.

No one had answers. The city blamed the contractors. The contractors turned it back on the city. Publicly, that is. Privately they ate and drank together at the finest restaurants, making merry and mocking the citizens.

They both pointed a finger at the Sewerage & Water Board. The City Council threatened to freeze the Public Works budget. Hipsters drank cocktails while standing in excavation hole rainwater up to their bric-a-brac jewelry and facial hair tomfoolery.

Was there an outcry? A March on City Hall? Citizens who'd had enough?

Only about the historic blue & white street name markers that were routinely broken and discarded by work crews. Other than that, as long as the Saints played and festivals were festin', as long as 2nd lines shook and Mardi Gras didn't get the hook, so be it. Let the streets lagoon and the roads resemble an archaeological dig. This is how is, so let the good times roll.

Maya was not in the mood to accept the unacceptable, though. Not tonight. The more martial arts classes she had with Sifu Julius Mosley and the more she improved herself, the less time and patience she had for low expectations. It was on her mind as she continued to roll her bike closer to home.

"Tired of this," she snapped.

10 BITTER WORDS TEACH EMPTINESS.

NO LAUGHING, NO CELEBRATION, AND NO CHILDLIKE JOY COULD top the lift in Vinh Nguyen's heart when he received the update from Cuong about the man upstairs called Tree. Nguyen had made him wait to tell about it until they were outside in the car. Sister Pat had already kept the restaurant open much later than usual, and even the boss didn't want to overextend her good grace.

They were on St. Bernard, heading away from downtown and the river on their way back home.

"That skinny little ratface Bao Vu won't know what hit him. First we take his queen. Make her disappear. Then his *mi dang*, Black, connection."

"They say 'the plug' now," Cuong corrected.

Nguyen scoffed.

"The pug? Like a little dog?"

"No *đại ca*, boss," said Cuong. "The plug, like plug your ears," he gestured with his right hand.

Nguyen wasn't abiding with that.

"The plug? What? His connection. We either take him or just shoot him. This I need to think about."

"You want me to handle it?"

"You? No, I need an enforcer," said Nguyen. "A man who can take care of the whole room. Wipe 'em out."

"But I can…"

Nguyen interrupted with, "Enough! Just drive! That's your job."

They had made a right turn on Claiborne and would typically veer over to the left for the on-ramp to I-10. But Cuong saw the car's dashboard giving him a warning.

"Okay, but we need to get gas. Very low," he said on his way to the closest gas station on Elysian Fields, a short distance away.

Nguyen's positive spirit was now deflated.

"We? You should have filled up the tank before I was in here. All you have to do is be my driver," he huffed.

"Sorry. My apologies. I didn't realize."

The next couple minutes were silent, and Cuong was happy to pull up to an open pump the furthest distance from the convenience store. There were two other cars under the canopy as well. A couple spots from them. Both cars had Florida plates. They were caravaning to their house rental following the steak dinner at Brassy.

Nguyen and Cuong scanned the area to see one person pumping gas for each car and three others inside each vehicle. Keeping them in easy eyesight was always Nguyen's preference. Cuong had parked back a bit since there was plenty of traffic moving on the streets around them. Keep out of easy view. He was about to get out of the car, but Nguyen grabbed his arm.

"Stop," said the older man with Vinnie menace as he pointed at the emerging scene.

11 WARRIORS ARE NATURAL.

MAYA LIKED TO BIKE IN THE BLOCKS WITH LIGHTS OR PEOPLE AT night. On streets with cars not driven by being pointed in a direction and the gas pedal jammed to the floor. Neither Claiborne nor Robertson was an option, so her route was to pass by the gas station before making a right at the sports bar on Derbigny. The former was well lit, and the latter usually had people coming and going. Back in the day, right up until she started staying with her Aunt Nekisha, it had been the type of club where NOPD would make a surprise visit if they wanted to clear a couple dozen warrants to look good for the news. Turned out it was run by a pharmacist whose pill mill was about five minutes away. When he went down, so did the club, but now with new owners it was tame other than the private thing they did upstairs. Mostly just packed on game day.

Aunt Nekisha hadn't told Maya everything. Not that the club which was shut down had been owned by Maya's parents, Franklin and Eugenia. Not what was revealed in the trial—that the walls could've come crumbling down for Maya at any point from 2nd grade until middle school since the Feds were investigating her parents that whole time.

But Maya knew the phrase "all assets seized" too well. She definitely knew her parents wouldn't walk free for another decade. In the aftermath of it all, she began fidgeting more than ever before. Constant hair twirling was next. Then the pulling out of hair that became an addiction.

Maya wondered if her daddy's knack and fondness for taking chances that often paid off was part of the reason he went down a road that almost guaranteed a long bid in a way-out-of-state federal pen. She also wondered if her accountant mommy's confidence at her ability with numbers led to the faulty overconfidence that she could manipulate the books to hide a mountain with a handkerchief.

This is what Maya had never told anyone. Why she dropped out of LSU after the first semester. Easier to just say that financial aid fell through. Was it true what was in her parents caused them to destroy themselves and their family? Maya wondered if she would do the same thing too.

Even worse, what if she didn't possess a special talent or anything that made her unique. These thoughts that often returned to her mind and danced around there were quickly dissolved by the sight to her right as she absently looked around.

Maya was learning from Sifu Mosley how to better observe, to read a person, to know in any situation how to handle them if it all went sour. The best way to reduce distance if they had a gun, and how to gain it if they had a knife, she was outnumbered, or when retreating. This was second to the ultimate goal of never having to fight in the first place.

Maya saw three cars parked at the gas station island. Two of them had out-of-state plates. The other vehicle was more isolated. Nothing atypical, but it was the two young men striding with purpose from the shadowy side of the gas station building that had her immediately putting her bike down and angling in that direction.

Their guns shone in the moonlight. Neither had been fired once before they were grabbed from car break-ins. At least three out of four stolen guns in New Orleans came about this way. The gunmen's style of black jeans as tight as leggings, multi-colored hair wrapped in bandanas, and skull tattoos were unintentionally as similar to the late 80s L.A. hair metal bands named on their t-shirts as could be. The comparison ended there.

Maya saw each of them walk up to the passenger side of a Florida car and pull on the handles to find they were locked.

"Get the fuck out. Alla you," yelled the guy closest to her.

Right after, the gunman furthest from Maya yelled, "You too. Heard me?" at those inside the other car. From her angle, she could see both people who had been pumping gas were ducking and trying to hide from what was about to go down.

"Dunno where this is coming from, but here we go," said Maya to herself. She didn't know exactly what she was going to do but had an unexpected inner push to get in the fray and make it happen.

Maya was sideways to the back of the thieves. They were so focused on those inside the cars that they didn't see her approaching. Yelling and swinging their sticks. Maya was now close enough to see they were so young and looked like little boys. Guns so new they looked like little toys. But this was no game. All about hitting an easy lick times two.

She didn't realize she should be nervous as she nonchalantly walked behind the first guy. This time she wasn't hesitant like she had been in City Park.

Wasn't fazed when he caught her in his periphery and spun to his right toward her as she took a few more steps toward his partner at the second car.

Maya wasn't worried about bullets as she saw the second gunman in front of her shaking his weapon at the car, then turning it and advancing left toward her. She had the duo where she wanted, sandwiching her and approaching with their guns in front of them. Guiding like flashlights in a cave. Maya in the middle.

The speed of everything around Maya instantly slowed in her mind. It became clear how she would handle the situation, like hidden knowledge she was now privy to, but she didn't consciously think of each step. Maya just felt the flow.

It felt completely natural to wait until they were an arm's length away, both to her left and to her right. Maya faced forward, tightened her fists at waist level, and quickly stepped wide to her left. As she did, she used the balance shift to swing her arms and fists hard like clock hands back to her left, up and under the chin of one pursuing gunman, briefly freezing him. In a continuous motion she completed the clockwise circle by arcing her arms high and back to her right as she shifted her weight in unison. When her fists came down on the head of the second gunman, he saw stars.

While they were both stunned and in pain, she took a big step with her left foot toward the second gunman and twisted to her right side. Made her left hand into a claw and grabbed his left wrist. Spun like a corkscrew back around to her left, twirled him across her body, and took a strong left step to let the momentum guide him straight into the other guy. Skull to skull. They both crumpled to the ground, knocked out.

Maya kicked both guns from their hands. The Florida visitors watched in shock from inside their cars, while Maya paused briefly to catch her breath. To onlookers, she appeared matter-of-fact while walking back to her bike, but Maya was in her head trying to figure out what just happened.

12 A VIEW CAN BE A GUIDE.

Vinh Nguyen had observed all of this. His eyes had a new Vinnie glint in them.

"Cuong, do you know what is *Fang Shu?*" he asked.

"Uh no. Is it…"

Nguyen truly didn't want an answer, only to expound a bit.

"It means what happens is meant to happen. Fate," he said. "You not getting gas, your foolishness, was meant to put us in this place to witness. She is not a man. She is *mi dang*, Black people, not one of us. But now I have seen my enforcer."

Cuong was speechless. Partly because he thought he had just previously showed his value. Partly because the stranger who was not Vietnamese was about to jump above him on the ladder. How could he save face when word got out?

"Follow her," said Nguyen. "Slowly."

"But the gas tank," cautioned Cuong.

"Later. Don't let her get out of your sight," said Nguyen to cut off any further discussion.

Cuong waited until Maya walked past their line of vision before slowly pulling forward. She was just ahead of them, pushing her bike, and turning on Derbigny. Cuong nosed the car onto Elysian Fields, keeping in the right lane.

13 VARY WHAT CAUSES HARM.

Tree, government name Kiri Price, was physically hurting and emotionally angry. He was standing in the bathroom washing blood from his face and arms. Hadn't expected the Vietnamese man who came to his door would be so quick and powerful. Tree had major advantage as far as height and range of arms and legs. But the man called Cuong knew to get in tight and neutralize all of this. Tree's gun too.

He couldn't believe what he was about to do. But hey, the game is grimy. Too often Tree felt like he was still in the mud, and this seemed like a better way out. Money is money. At least that's what he was telling himself to neutralize the steady voice inside that alternated saying, "You done fucked up," with "Sell out."

Tree was about to walk over to the refrigerator, one that had the smell of sitting through one too many power outages, and grab something from the freezer to put on the bruise by his right eye.

A light knock at the door shifted and quickened his stride in that direction. Tree was on edge and ready to snap. Didn't care who it was.

He grabbed a baseball bat along the way, the one he couldn't get to before Cuong put the hurt on him. He wanted to take it out on somebody. If it was Cuong again, then chin check time was coming. Didn't matter what new allegiance he made. Just evening up the score. Getting his lick back. Eye for an eye.

Tree's aching head bobbed as his knees rose high to the door, steady like a metronome. He flung it open with his left hand and immediately turned to his right in baseball swinging stance, ready to hit whatever moved. Simultaneously he called out.

"Play with me, ya gonna pay, motherfucker. Hear me?"

There was no assassin or anyone waiting to do him harm on the other side of the door. Just two pretty young women who were scared and jumped back as a furious Tree quickly blew air through his teeth and moved into the doorway.

"Scram, bitches," spat Tree.

The shorter of the two stepped forward as she responded.

"Who you calling a bitch?"

Tree dropped the bat to his side.

"You, uglass bitch."

The one who had knocked on the door stepped between them.

"Hey, hey, Brit!" to her friend and, "Kiri, didn't you get my text? What happened to you?" to Tree.

"Don't mind me. Go 'way," as he turned to go inside and close the door on them.

Brittany spoke up again as she stepped past her friend.

"Oh my God. We're here for business. Calling people bitches. You don't know me."

Tree turned to come after her. For the second time, the woman who had brought Brittany there tried to mediate."

"Brit, shut up. Kiri, just real quick. Please?"

He was angry at everything, but she looked good to him. He softened a bit.

"Please," she said for the second time, though as a statement, not a question.

"Alright," he said. "Since you asked with manners. Right quick."

Tree continued inside but left the door open.

Flora Mosley spoke softly and quickly to Brittany.

"Stay out here. I'm getting some sniff. Smiles too so we can trip."

Brittany was aghast and mouthed her words.

"You're going in there with him?"

"Yes," said Flora. "Cash," she commanded.

"Oh my God. Tell ya boy to learn some manners," but Brittany complied.

Flora stepped inside Tree's apartment and closed the door.

"I'd ask you to sit, but…"

The place was a mess. The couch would have been the only option, but it had fresh blood on it. Flora stayed standing.

"What you want?" he asked.

"Finally," she thought. Today wasn't a day to make the usual small talk up front.

"We're gonna party, so a gram of coke and a couple Smiles."

Tree looked impressed.

"You graduating from those baby bumps. Gram, huh? That'll cost you. 'Course we can work something out."

She knew what he meant. Beneath the bruises and blood, his look and tone were as obvious and suggestive as could be.

"I can pay for it. What are we looking at?" she said, keeping it matter-of-fact.

Tree persisted. "I know what I'm looking at. You probably never had some good D up in ya. Pretty Uptown girl don't know what you missing."

In the same voice as before, she said, "Kiri, how much? I gotta boyfriend."

He sniffed, curled his mouth, and sighed.

"That don't matter. Alright. For you, gram $200. $25 each Smiles pill."

Flora nodded and opened her purse to count the money without removing it. Once she had the $250, she held it out.

Tree pulled a backpack from under the couch and took out a pill container along with a small bag that held a gram of cocaine.

14 YOU DON'T SEE STRATEGY.

THE FIRST BLOCK ON DERBIGNY THAT MAYA TOOK TO WALK her bike while Vinh Nguyen and Cuong tailed was relatively quiet. From Marigny to Mandeville was another story. As usual, lots of people hanging out. Drugged out zombies stumbling, passed out, or ready for more. Music pumping. Always somebody yelling. 24-hour corner store fueling it. Cheap liquor, hard drugs, and high-powered guns sold like snacks inside and steps away. At the counter, glass tubes for smoking crack or meth.

The sidewalk and street in front of Jim's Meat Market was littered with so many colorful paper roses tossed out of the tubes it looked like a flowery carpet to the abyss. Scouring pad pieces also conveniently available at the counter were used as a filter. This corner store, like others in New Orleans, was known for open air drug dealing. NOPD let it go on, unless there was a murder or night out against crime photo op, which forced the zombies and good timers to tuck away into the shadows.

Despite all of this, Maya still preferred the route compared to proceeding up Mandeville from Claiborne. This was the devil she knew. And they mostly left her alone, knowing she wasn't passing through to buy. She said nothing and made no eye contact.

Nguyen watched from their vantage point half a block back. With Cuong's slow pace, various people began to walk up to the car, thinking, naturally, they were there to buy drugs.

"Don't stop, but don't drive too fast," ordered Nguyen.

Cuong pointed ahead of them as Maya turned on Mandeville and walked her bicycle from the sidewalk to the street. They didn't see her drop the objects she took out of her pocket. By the time the car passed slowly through the people and turned right, there was no sight of Maya. But a sudden sound jolted them. An immediate flat tire. Nguyen looked first at Cuong, then to his right and saw Maya's bike laying on the sidewalk. Neither this block nor the next had operating street lights. Just lit people and the cacophony from Jim's. "What the fuckity fuck?" wondered Nguyen.

"Oh, no. Flat tire. Gas is almost empty," said Cuong. He knew this wasn't the place to be stranded.

Nguyen reached over to backhand him.

"Useless. Get out and fix it."

Cuong tentatively stepped outside. They were near the corner, but no one had noticed yet that the car had stopped. Shortly after he took a few steps, something hard struck him in the head. He called out in pain and rushed back inside, hand to his forehead.

"What you doing?" asked Nguyen.

"They're after us. Somebody shot me," said Cuong.

Nguyen leaned toward him. "Are you kidding me. It's just a welt. Coward."

Vinh Nguyen was about to push him back out but instead stepped out of the car himself. He too was promptly hit in the head by a hard object. He covered his head with his arms and looked around. Someone must be hiding between the houses. Maybe under.

"Show yourself. Who is this?" he said to the sky.

Again he was struck. This time dinging his right arm. Nguyen winced. He had a gun, but it was in the car.

A voice called out, "Why are you following me?"

Nguyen couldn't tell where the voice was coming from, but his immediate anger subsided as he realized it had to be her. His enforcer to be.

"I gotta reason," he said.

For the third time he was thumped with something that hurt. This time to the left side of his stomach.

"I'm trying to tell you."

He paused to see if another was coming. The objects seemed to be flying from all sides.

"If this is the uh young lady from the gas station, I saw how you handled those uh robbers. I want to hire you."

Maya's response was immediate.

"Don't need a job."

Nguyen swiveled his head to find the origin of the disembodied voice. Kept going around then back the other way.

"I pay very good money. Hire you to be my bodyguard."

"I said, don't need a job."

He persisted. "Can we talk face to face?"

"No," said Maya. Nguyen was a persistent man, and this was no different.

"You knowing we were tailing you proves my point. This would be perfect for you," he said. "Just think about it."

He reached into his pocket with one hand while

reluctantly dropping the other arm protecting his head. Hunched down a bit to reduce the target of his body as if that would help.

"Here's my card. Putting it there. Vinh Nguyen is my name. I'm a very good businessman." He crouched to the ground and dropped his business card.

Maya still didn't trust him.

"Leave," she said.

Nguyen realized this was the best he could get for now and that it was best to fix the flat at the gas station if he wanted to keep his car.

"Thank you, miss. Please think about my offer. Very good money."

There was no further response from Maya. Nguyen looked around one last time before getting back into the car. Cuong left for the gas station. Once Maya could see their lights turning onto Claiborne, she climbed down from the tree near where the car had been. She grabbed the business card, pocketed it, and pulled her bike upright to finish the walk a few more doors to her aunt's place. The pennies she'd thrown at the two men were left where they were.

15 SLOW DOWN AND CALM YOUR MIND.

Julius and Samira Mosley both had a morning ritual. Upon waking, he would flip randomly through *The Last Shadow* book for an entry to start the day. She would turn on the morning news to stay on top of things. As with all couples, the end of the night and the beginning of the day could easily be thorny hurdles to overcome.

They'd been in the groove for a solid 20 years. Julius had a hair more than a decade on Samira as far as age. As is often the case, that suited them well. Samira was an old soul, wiser than her years might indicate. Julius was no slouch himself, but cats & dogs, yin & yang, and couples are built differently. The marked maturity is often in the favor of those with the 2 X chromosomes. They both knew it.

This Monday kept to a routine. When the alarm clock struck 8:00 a.m., with the sound of Roy Ayers on the vibes, they first greeted each other. Next, Julius reached for the book on his nightstand. Samira grabbed the TV remote from hers. Since her favorite news channel was on commercial, Julius read aloud.

"Slow down and calm your mind."

"That first part sounds exactly like life in New Orleans."

"The first part does," he said. "But there aren't many calm minds here."

She pushed back a bit. "More than you think."

"Can't be that way if you party at the drop of a hat."

"Julius."

He changed direction.

"What time did the kids get in?"

"A.J. was back before I came to bed," she said. "Flora was…later. I checked her room in the night."

"In the night?" asked Julius, growing agitated. He pulled the covers back to get up.

"I'm going to talk to her right…"

Samira interrupted and gestured toward the TV with a tilt of her head.

"Wait. Sssh."

The weathercaster Julie Cormier was standing to the side of a hurricane tracking map. The arc of the path from the Gulf of Mexico to landfall showed New Orleans a little too close for comfort, as was often the case.

"Tropical Storm Izzy is expected to be Hurricane Izzy by tomorrow. Category 1 at most, but that can still do major damage, as we know. At this point Izzy will make landfall Wednesday night. New Orleans, it looks like we'll escape a direct hit. It's a small quick moving storm, but the question that remains is how close does it get? Start your hurricane precautions now. Be prepared. Tune in for further updates," she said before handing it over to the morning news anchors.

Julius and Samira turned and looked at each other. He spoke.

"I'll start bringing in my things out back. But first."

He left the bed and walked down the hallway to Flora's room. It was no surprise she was sound asleep.

"Flora."

No response. "Flora," he said louder.

She moved around a bit and pulled the covers over her head. He stepped closer and yanked them back just as quickly.

"Unnnnnnh. What are you doing?"

"Flora, get up. Now."

"Daddy, let me sleep."

"No. Up."

She sat up and wasn't happy about it.

"What did you do last night?" he started.

"I went out with Brittany," she said. "Dancing. Didn't stay out all night. Had two beers."

"Just two beers? Nothing else?"

"You're being cringe. What do you mean?"

He went at it from a different angle.

"Okay. What time you get in?"

Flora had long known the benefit of stretching her words out, giving her a little more time to concoct a response.

"Ummmmm, liiiiike 2 or 3, but I don't have to be anywhere today. Just need to get my textbooks online."

He was skeptical.

"Flora, you're my daughter. I love you dearly. But so help me if there's anything you aren't telling me."

"I know, daddy. I'm a college student on summer break having fun. Don't stress. I'm careful."

Julius softened a bit and took her hand.

"Alright, thanks for putting up with your dad."

He kissed her hand and left the room. She wiped her nose, reached under her pillow for her phone, and texted Brittany.

"Don't come over. Daddy detective. Be by later," it read.

16 GHOSTS AND SPIRITS WILL RISE.

Ms. Nekisha Fisher's mornings, and therefore those of her niece Maya, were anything but leisurely. Rise and shine, it's cleaning time. Typically Ms. Nekisha wasn't due at the new VA hospital on Canal Street until mid-afternoon, 2nd shift, but today was long. Co-worker on vacation. As far as Maya, she often left early for extra hours at either Brassy or the restaurant in the Marriott at Canal and Chartres, which meant she'd eventually bike off to martial arts class in City Park before heading back for the French Quarter dinner crowd.

Fisher had recently posted for and received the bump away from 1st shift as part of her promotion, and she was basking in the reality of Maya's much younger knees and back. Old houses in New Orleans always settled unevenly. Had been for a century or more. This meant a steady supply of mystery dust. Not to mention the bugs of every type who loved to sneak inside during the summer to escape the heat, same as humans.

Maya was already wearing one of her mother's wigs and armed with a large bottle of all-purpose cleaner and paper towels to work on the kitchen. She checked the nearest clock to see she would have a reprieve in twelve minutes to bike off to work for a shift at the hotel restaurant, thanks to her neighbor Mr. Charles who was handy with patching bike tires.

She didn't expect to hear what came next.

"Oh, no. Oh, hell no!"

Maya left her supplies on the counter and rushed out the front door.

"Auntie Kish, what's the…oh."

Fisher was wearing nurse scrubs and holding the trash bag she'd taken outside. That was no surprise. But she was standing next to a "For Sale" sign planted in the front yard of the home she rented. It felt like an insult. She was angry and her eyes glowed.

"After seventeen years, this is how they're gonna do me. No. It's not right. Where's my phone?"

She rushed inside.

Maya stayed in place and saw layers of life flip through her mind. She went to a scene when she was in middle school and pictured herself climbing the same tree she'd gone up in when Vinh Nguyen and his driver were following her the night before.

Aunt Nekisha was on the porch watching her. "Girl, you're a regular Tarzan zipping up and down that tree. But hear, be careful, baby."

"I'm fine. Done it a million times, Aunt Kish. Come try."

The shaking of head from side to side to indicate "no way" seemed to extend beyond that which a neck was capable of stretching.

"Look, I'd fall on my tail and take a couple of branches with me doing what you're doing," the older lady scoffed.

Maya urged her. "C'mon, try it."

"My baby, best believe these feet are staying on the ground."

This time Maya paused and spoke differently,

"Auntie, you must."

Fisher's eyes got wide and she looked in the other direction.

"Baby, how'd you do that? I see you right there but it sounded like it came from up the street."

Maya laughed. "A ventriloquist came to my school last week. She showed us how to talk without moving our lips and throw our voice too. Makes it sound distant. I've been practicing."

"I'll be. You sure got me."

Maya returned to present day, threw away the trash bag, and hurried inside. Her Aunt was on the phone.

"I know, but I've done right by you," she stressed. "Wasn't late on rent even once, Mr. Al."

Maya had a sense of the response when Aunt Nekisha eventually said, "Maybe I want to buy it too. Been here long enough. Got roots."

Ms. Nekisha was biting her lip not to talk over the landlord and what she viewed as his petty justification for unacceptable behavior. She wouldn't let this fly from a younger person. Even an elder could be out of line, and no notice given qualified as that.

"Really? Alright. Yes, sir. But…"

Maya could tell the landlord's side of the call was getting shorter each time.

"You think it'd be that much?" asked Aunt Nekisha. "I understand. Goodbye, Mr. Al."

She was about to explode. First came a deep breath, eyes closed, and only after a handful of seconds passed did she paste a look of composure on her face.

"What'd he say?" Maya asked, but she already knew.

The barely concealed politeness from the phone call melted away.

"This trifling man had no apology or the good sense that he should have told me in advance. Didn't even think I would want to buy this place. I no longer serve his purpose, I'm disposable. We're disposable."

"Why don't you buy it?" asked Maya.

"My credit's not bad. Maya," said Aunt Nekisha, "He thinks down payment and closing costs would come to as much as $20 to $30,000. Maybe more."

At that, Maya was astonished. "So much?"

"As if anybody in New Orleans makes enough to put away that kinda money. I'm getting paid way better now as an RN than I did as an LPN, but it hasn't been long enough yet for me to save that much."

"I'll pick up more shifts," Maya offered.

"Baby girl, I appreciate you." The love and pain in Aunt Nekisha's eyes were palpable. "I told your parents I'd take care of you. Feels like you're the one taking care of me."

"Aunt Kish," said Maya.

"I just think, no disrespect, that would be too little, too late. Most likely new owner would want to live here, not rent it to us, Mr. Al said. We gotta look at getting together enough for a deposit and a couple months' rent to find a new place."

She paused and swung an index finger to point off to her left. "Block closer you get to the corner is hot, but at least we know it. They know us too. Maybe we find something cheaper further out. 'Course that means longer drive for me and bike for you."

Ms. Nekisha sighed.

"We'll figure this out. Our people always do."

Before continuing, she clenched her fists.

"They try to aggravate us. Intimidate. Wear us down. But we always figure it out. Now I got to get myself to the hospital before I'm late."

She grabbed her keys and left. After hearing the car start up and leave, Maya thought for a minute. Off to her room she went. The pants she was wearing last night were in the top of the laundry basket.

Maya lifted them up and dug in the right front pocket for Vinh Nguyen's business card. She studied it intently.

She looked in the mirror, remembering when she couldn't stand to see herself. Not in photos or even in the eyes of others. Shortly after her parents were taken away, it started with one hair. Next she pulled out a few and chewed on the ends. It soon became so impulsive and pervasive that kids at school asked if she'd gotten a haircut. Aunt Nekisha didn't know what to think. Was it alopecia? Maya was too embarrassed to admit to her that she'd been pulling out her own hair.

By the time Maya was at LSU, she randomly came upon the term trichotillomania and self-diagnosed herself as having it. She started shaving her head once a month and wearing a wig. Oh, did her mother have a wide collection. This helped with lapsing, because it wasn't real hair to pull and chew. But it brought on questions galore in the dorm. Was her shaved head about empowerment? Health issues? Since her aunt had mentioned alopecia, where hair would fall out from stress, Maya would just tell people she was dealing with something heavy.

Truth be told, her financial aid only dropped off because she didn't fill out necessary paperwork. Fear of people and the public had her wanting to return home to spend days alone in her room at Aunt Nekisha's.

17 VIRTUES BRING EXPANSION.

THE MAN SNOOZING IN HIS SPACIOUS BED WITH A BY-THE-HOUR beauty on either side of him was as arrogant as he was young. His apartment was stylish but impersonal. From abstract art paintings to uncomfortable modern furniture. It looked staged. And it was. An interior designer picked out everything from A-Z for him. He just paid the bill with a young man's hubris and an old man's wallet. His name was Bao Vu.

He was not happy to be woken by a phone call. Even in the afternoon. Even from his right-hand man.

"Better have a reason, Teo."

Teo wasn't intimidated. They came up together. Were like brothers.

"I got one," he said. "Hurricane coming. Shipment from Houston on Wednesday night might get delayed."

"Then get it here tomorrow. No delays," pushed Bao Vu.

Teo explained. "Meth they got now, but those keys of heroin not expected in Houston 'til Wednesday. What I'm supposed to do about rushing it through Mexico?"

"Fuck!" boomed Bao Vu. Neither woman budged. Night had stretched into day, liquor flowed, and the bumps were bumping, so they were in dreamland.

He continued, "How can I set up shop with Q like this? Fuck, Teo. I already know what he's gonna say. And you should know--they don't want meth in the 7th ward.

That's white people shit."

A text came through from Cai, Bao Vu's girlfriend.

"OMW," it read.

At this he shook the two women next to him.

"Out, out" he ordered.

Neither of them said anything, just quietly rose to get dressed and leave. Glad to, since they were being paid for the rest of the day.

"What?" asked Teo.

"Don't worry about it. I gotta figure this shit out."

Bao Vu hung up and promptly locked the front door behind his visitors. He walked across the open loft to the balcony door and opened it. The air felt good as usual in the lead up to a hurricane. He grabbed the pack of cigarettes and lighter he kept nearby to have a smoke and look at the sky while he thought about the situation.

18 UNITY COMES IN MANY FORMS.

Julius Mosley had a half-sized class with him in City Park. No Maya, which was surprising. He knew she worked two jobs, but he also hadn't known her to miss a single session. Her drive and example lifted the others, so today felt almost lackluster by comparison.

"Let's finish today off with fist push-ups," he announced. "All weight on the first two knuckles. At least 20 reps. See if you can hit more. Maya say to anyone she wouldn't be here today?"

The students shook their heads no and dropped to the grass. Sifu counted them off. A car with its stereo rocking pulled up. The lyrics were clear. The music was smooth. The song was one of those rare ones that most everyone liked.

Softly slowly turn,
Fumbling for the key,
Walked so far to hear,
Walked so far to see.

Flora and Brittany sang and moved along to the same song while they sat high and tripping in Brittany's room.

Crooked buildings there,
She who was a room,
Passed her time in words,
Spent her mind in dreams.

Bao Vu had also turned on the radio and heard it while he repeatedly called and texted Cai. She hadn't shown up.

This wasn't like her. He was displeased. Mostly the lack of control was what irritated him, as in his control of her.

When it is time you'll see
A sweet light in a dark room,
And where you lay your head
A hidden stream will be.

Julius Mosley and his students were finishing up.

"Good job, everyone. See you tomorrow. Probably no Wednesday class, but let's see what path the hurricane takes."

Step before me now,
Dusty creaking stairs,
Future is behind you,
Past is happening still.
Open up the door,
A rickety array,
The shadows haunt my mind,
And some of them scorch my fingers.
When it is time you'll see
A sweet light in a dark room,
And where you lay your head
A hidden stream will be.
And where you lay your head
A hidden stream will be.

With that, the car drove off.

19 FISH AND BIRDS HAVE DIFFERENT COURSES.

Vinh Nguyen was a man who spoke in riddles, occasionally responded in an unexpected way, and didn't like to answer questions. All of this and more was his recipe for toying with people to keep them on their toes.

Though he had immediately seen Maya as his needed enforcer, he certainly wasn't going to tell her that. Incrementalism was his way. Bait and switch too. And his eyes showed no tells.

Nguyen was sitting at his desk across from Maya. She seemed eager enough for him to get his verbal talons into her. She wouldn't have come otherwise. Tell her what she wanted to hear. Seal the deal.

"Why do you need a bodyguard? You have him," Maya said, gesturing at Cuong who was standing behind her.

Nguyen, as usual, made it up as he went, schmoozing as Vinh Nguyen, the businessman.

"Cuong is my driver. He needs a gun. You have your hands. You are the weapon. I saw what you did at the gas station."

Flattery was always effective.

"Thank you," said Maya. "I have a lot to learn but… how do I say this? No disrespect, sir. It's not usual that somebody who looks like you would want to work with somebody who looks like me."

She'd been trying not to stare at the bottle on Nguyen's desk but couldn't resist and saw that, yes, there was indeed a dead snake in the liquid. Was it a cobra?

He had wondered if she would bring up the racial component.

"That is correct. I am a fish and you are a bird. You are an exceptional bird. Despite your skepticism, you still came out here to talk about it. How about this as an advance to ease your mind? I am a fish who can pay you well. 10 bands to show I'm serious," he said.

Maya watched him casually open his desk drawer and take out a banded stack of cash as if he did it often. He tossed it underhand to her once he saw her eyes show hesitation turned to acceptance. As he extended his arm, she saw a part of a "D" tattooed on his hand. Any remaining reluctance she had melted away upon holding what looked like 100 $100 bills

"Um, I'm sorry about the flat tire," she volunteered.

Nguyen was pleased. He'd figured as much or at least had hoped for it from her.

Cuong on the other hand was angry at this confirmation that she was the reason he had been on his hands and knees at the gas station fixing the tire after tailing her.

"Of course," Nguyen praised. "Useful. Resourceful. Now you see why I knew you'd be perfect."

"No guns," stressed Maya.

"As you wish."

"Don't mean to sound ungrateful, but…"

Nguyen knew enough to know that starting a sentence that way meant a statement of exactly that was sure to come. Weariness crept into his voice. "What is it?"

"I really appreciate all this, but is there a way to make more money? My Aunt needs it."

Nguyen felt smug and pleased. Now he knew her motivation. Time for knives out, in a manner of speaking. He kept his mouth closed for a moment. Didn't want to so obviously bare teeth and show her Vinnie yet.

"We're just beginning, Maya. If you're in, though…"

His pause was so long that Cuong smirked at the ridiculousness of it all teeter-tottering on the end of a cliff.

"Are you in?" asked Nguyen, tip-toeing toward the edge.

"Yes, yes," said Maya.

"Too easy," thought Nguyen.

He looked over Maya's head to Cuong. "She did take the money."

Back to Maya. "Here's to fish and birds. To swimming and flying. Now, my dear, a little walk." She was on her way to the abyss, but she didn't yet know it.

The three of them exited out the back door. Nguyen's former jewelry store was in the middle of a strip mall. He led the group past two back doors before stopping at the third and unlocking the metal door.

It took Maya a few seconds for her eyes to adjust from the bright sun to the few fading bulbs still producing a faint bit of light in the empty retail space. Musty bordering on moldy was in effect, mixed with the palpable essence of fear.

There were two chairs in the space. Jimmy, his nose bandaged, sat bored at one. Happy for company. A woman, disheveled and terrified, was in the other, bound and gagged. She had been put together meticulously before the abduction, but now she looked like she'd been through a nightmare.

"Here is my problem," said Nguyen. He was matter-of-fact in such a way to show complete control. "Thought she could steal from me, Vinh Nguyen."

The woman in the chair shook her head vigorously to deny it.

Cuong said under his breath but with emphasis, "*Đại ca*, boss. Your name."

"It doesn't matter what she hears. Everyone knows who I am."

To Maya, continuing his performance with a hint of faux sadness. "Stole, betrayed me, harmed my family. She and Bao Vu."

"No, no," came through the blue rag as unintelligible, but Cai, Bao Vu's girlfriend, tried anyway.

"Maya, you need to make more money quickly," said Nguyen. "Here's your first job. Your test."

"You want me to…?"

"Yes, it is unfortunate it's come to this. But necessary."

Cai directed all her efforts toward Maya. Pleaded with her eyes.

Hoping that not every word would be muffled, she said, "It's not true. Help me, please." Unfortunately, none of it came through with any clarity.

Maya hadn't expected any of this and it was all overwhelming.

"I need to think about it," she said. "I've never done anything like that before."

Nguyen locked eyes with her. No blinking. No breaking his gaze.

"My dear, you're in. We have an agreement. You took the money. Another 10 bands when you handle her. Go get some rest. Come back in two days. Here's to fish and birds."

He stepped over to Cuong who mouthed "Two days?" at him.

"I need to enjoy myself," Nguyen discreetly hissed back.

He gestured to exit. Cuong walked a concerned and confused Maya to the same door they initially came through. He was already thinking about the best way to dispose of Cai before this Maya person arrived. He knew that making Vinh Nguyen think it was his own idea was always the best tack.

After they exited, Nguyen moved closer to Cai. Time to let Vinnie loose.

His face showed only contempt and malevolence.

Con đĩ, bitch, you are here for one reason." He leaned in. "Bao Vu. Your boyfriend. I was going to send you to the East Coast to be fucked by strangers all day. You're serving another purpose instead." He smiled with a sneer. "Now I can have her kill you and it will never come back on me. Very convenient. They will believe the Blacks in New Orleans are capable of anything. But Bao Vu? I myself will kill him where he stands."

Nguyen turned to Jimmy.

"Go back to the office."

Next, he ran his fingertips across Cai's face.

"I've been waiting for this."

Nguyen stepped back and unzipped his pants.

20 PROTECT YOURSELF WITH COMMUNICATION.

The tension inside the 7 Bells Barber Shop between Duels and Hope on Monday night was thick as fog. Heavy as humidity. It wasn't from men waiting to get lined up and arguing over a top five list. These four, two in barber chairs on each side, were discussing business. Or at least one on each side was. The other two were there just in case. Nobody was reclining. It wasn't that kind of sit down.

"Like I told you on the phone," said Bao Vu. "If a hurricane blows through on Wednesday, I won't be able to get the shipment from Houston."

"Deal's a deal," said Quincy Adams who went by Q.

"I'm trying my best to fulfill it. But I can't control the weather."

To the point, Q responded. "You can control your people." He added, "Say, bruh. Where you from?"

Both Bao Vu and Teo bristled at this. They'd heard it all before.

"I was born and raised in New Orleans just like you. 9th ward off Chef in the East," spat out Bao Vu.

"Alright then," said Q. "Why you don't know this the 7th ward here, and if Izzy hits, don't matter if Tropical Storm or Cat 5? Power be out for at least a week. They be wantin' that dope too. Lots of it. Drug panic. Fiends feenin'."

At that, Kiri Price, known as Tree, nodded in agreement.

Q continued. "I'ma give it to 'em and make bookoo bucks. Handle your shit or we gotta problem." He knew he had a position of power, not just because they were in his barbershop where he liked to conduct business after hours.

Bao Vu paused. He was as suspicious of them as they were of him. A flicker of an idea appeared in his mind. It quickly expanded like a car's airbag until it pushed everything else out of his head. He spoke on it.

"Wait a minute. This is how you do business? You kidnap my girlfriend to hold it over me?"

Q rose in his chair, trying to extend his height well above a modest 5'2".

"What the fuck you talkin' 'bout? I look like I grab females off the street?"

Bao Vu didn't read the room or the person. He had no belief in Q. Just knew that now he was asserting, he didn't have to be defensive about a late delivery.

"Then who did? How do I know I can trust you?" he scoffed.

Q stood up, stretched up, and walked tall as he could over to Bao Vu who stayed seated but gestured at Teo, who took out his gun. Tree did the same.

Q spoke calmly and looked Bao Vu eye to eye. "We good?" was his loaded question.

Bao Vu tried to match the menace. "We good?" he replied.

Q held his stare a few seconds more before waving both gunmen off and stepping back. It wasn't going down like that. Not this time anyway. He hadn't grown up not knowing when the power would be on or where the next meal was coming from to go out like this.

"Handle your man," he said to Bao Vu. In his mind he was thinking that hell was coming to anyone who dared call him short, tiny, or any of the names he'd heard when he had no power. He was paranoid he might still get called any of them.

Bao Vu took a deep breath, which pushed away enough of the suspicions in his mind. He gave Teo the eye to put away his piece. Tree slowly followed suit.

Q made himself clear as could be to Bao Vu.

"Muthafucka, you came to me. How do I know I can believe a word you say?"

Bao Vu stood up, not breaking his gaze right back at Q.

"I'm doing the best I can."

"Sit your ass down. Pay 'em more to drive it in," said Q. "Don't care 'bout no weather."

"Bigger cut."

"Nah, YOUR problem. You trippin'."

Bao Vu knew this was how the meeting would go down, but that didn't help at the current moment. If he was in Q's shoes, he'd be talking the same. But he couldn't lose face that he was a pushover.

"If it gets delayed in Mexico, that's my fault too? Or the boat from Asia"

He was reaching and he knew it.

"Man, I don't need no Discovery Channel here," scoffed Q. "Get me the shit on Wednesday…" He smacked his hands together once while speaking. "Like." A second time. "We." And a third. "Agreed." Deep breath. "If not, I gotta problem. With you." He said it again. "With you. Say that about your woman again? I gotta 'nother problem with you. This meeting's over."

He added to Kiri, "Get that door right quick."

Tree loped to the door and unlocked it. Bao Vu and Teo looked at each other. Q had turned his back on them. They said no more and left. Tree firmly locked the door.

At that Q spoke. "Weird ass Chinese. I got finest of the fine females checkin' for me. Grab his bitch? He needs my connections, not the other way 'round. Wanna be the plug? Then be the muthafuckin' plug. Otherwise not rockin' with you."

Tree added, "Yeah, dude's weird. Why you need him?"

"Bruh, you need to read more. All this good synthetic shit coming from China. He be the plug for that."

Kiri didn't know what he meant, but he nodded as if he did.

Q squinted. "Tree."

"Yeah."

"Heard anything about it? His woman?"

"Me?"

"Anybody else in the room?" asked Q.

"Nah, nah. Ain't heard streets talking on it, but he got different streets, Q."

"Alright," agreed Q. "Pointin' a finger at me when he can't handle his shit."

Kiri paused.

"I gotta hit the men's," he said. "Lemme holla at you later."

"Yeah, get my ass outta here," said Q, though he knew their standard routine was both leaving at the same time for security-sake.

They dapped, Q went to the front door, unlocked it, and left. Tree took a deep breath and put his hands on the top of his head. Things were weighing heavily on him. He turned. Watching Q walking to his truck out on New Orleans St. was too much.

Parked on the street, Jimmy and Cuong looked at each other and nodded as they saw Q leave the barber shop. Time for them to get to work.

21 HAVE GREAT MEANING OR EMPTINESS.

Danh Trang and his mother Lan sat watching the news in a modest one-story ranch house on My Viet Drive. It was the home he'd grown up in. Mary Queen of Vietnam Church that many in the neighborhood attended was a stone's throw away. It was a tight knit community. He knew them and they knew him. Weathercaster Julie Cormier was giving them and many others the Tuesday morning update.

"Izzy became Hurricane Izzy overnight. Still at Category 1," she said. "Potentially quick intensification before landfall, but, if so, a quick drop back to what we see now. Izzy is a big enough storm that even with the path to the west of New Orleans, we can still expect damaging winds."

The two of them reached out and squeezed each other's hands.

"No mandatory evacuation is expected, other than that the parishes closer to the Gulf of Mexico especially need to prepare to evacuate or hunker down."

The news continued while Lan shrugged.

"Nothing we haven't seen before," she said.

"I'll cover the plants tonight." Danh paused. "But for now…"

His mother beamed, "I'm so proud of you. I wish your father could see this day."

"I don't know for sure yet," he cautioned.

"A mother knows. This was meant to happen. Especially when your name means success. Fame too."

Danh smiled and tilted his head.

"Whoa, whoa. Wait 'til later to see if I made you proud."

"You already have," she said. "I wish it was closer, of course, but I understand."

"If I stayed around here, I'd either have to rent from Vinh Nguyen or pay him not to get robbed. I've been driving to the other side of New Orleans anyway. Metairie drive's about the same."

Lan Trang's eyebrows angled and her mouth pursed.

"Vinh Nguyen all smiles and nice talk, but it's false. Bian Vu never should have given him a job."

"Bian Vu who runs the rice fields?" asked a stunned Danh.

"Yes," she confirmed. "You're about to turn 30, so it must have been a year or two before you were born. Vinh Nguyen showed up out of nowhere. He was quiet then, but I could see the bad in his eyes. He worked for Bian Vu until he beat up another worker in the fields."

Danh hadn't closed his mouth from surprise.

"The businessman Vinh Nguyen?",

"Oh yes. Then the whispers began over time. That he bought a building and doubled the rent. That he had 800 roosters fighting for money. The drugs. What happened to young women. Men who spoke out..."

She threw up her hands. "Enough of this."

"Seems like he's been running things forever," said Danh.

"He was running from something when he came here," said Lan. "Bad is bad. I want to rest my thoughts on other things. You stay away from him."

"Hmm. I'll keep my distance same as always. Wish me luck."

His mother hugged him and walked over to the shrine.

"Did you already talk to him?" she asked, meaning Danh's father, whose photo was leaning next to the Buddha figurine.

"Yes."

"Good boy. Now I will too."

Lan lit incense and kneeled, as Danh left for his appointment. She looked back in pain at the door now between them.

"He can never know. I can't lose him too," she said to her late husband, Phat.

Danh Trang's route was a frustrating one to him, same as many others all over New Orleans. For much of the year, a long stretch of Michoud had been torn up and the road work not completed. Discarded tires had been dumped and piling up for years closer to the swamps, but during the road construction months, many trying to zip along Michoud down to and beyond the subdivision with street names of high hopes, had been silent protesting by unloading their trash when they had to turn back. Expedition, Founders, Endeavors, Adventure, Horizon, Intrepid, Explorers, and Wayfarer were the promise. A virtual landfill near doorsteps was the reality.

This meant he and all the other neighbors had to loop back the other direction to Alcee Fortier, past the strip malls of markets, various businesses, empty buildings and more before taking Chef to 510 and zipping up to the highway.

While on this route, he saw Vinh Nguyen and Cuong getting out of a car parked in front of the jewelry store where it was known Nguyen kept his office. Trang slowed down to gauge him with new eyes from his mother's information. With a strange sense, Nguyen seemed to realize he was being watched. He turned back to see a startled Trang, who promptly sped up.

22 CHANGE WILL HAPPEN. TRYING TO RESIST IT IS LIKE RESISTING SUNRISE.

The Mid-City intersection where Queen Trini Lisa restaurant was located drew eyes upward before going inside. Like with many other streets, newcomers and visitors loved the folk art quality of the hand-painted signs. Not all realized there had been no street signs for almost two decades, so Chef had her daughter make them. Solomon fit on the small piece of wood, but D'Hemecourt had to have multiple lines to squeeze it in. The citizens of New Orleans were essentially the underfunded Public Works department, and with arguably greater effectiveness.

Chef Lisa had been in the small well-organized kitchen since 6:30 a.m. prepping for the day. Mixing up a big bowl of bara dough for the doubles, the restaurant's most popular item. Also, cooking up curry chicken, cabbage, chickpeas, jerk chicken, and more. Making sure plenty of the three main sauces were poured into small containers and placed in the cooler.

Despite the fact that Chef wasn't yet halfway through her 16-hour day, she had the true energy and pride of a restaurateur in her element. Even though it was lunch rush and there was a packed house, the personal touch was still key.

"Tables 4 and 6 are almost done. I'm gonna pop out real quick," Chef announced to the Prep Cook Cherelle, who was busy balling up bara dough, flattening it, frying it for a minute and a half, and then stacking it in a cooler to stay warm. She was hustling to do this while waiting on plantains cooking in the deep fryer for Table 5's plates.

On her way through the kitchen, Chef Lisa silenced the now-beeping fryer vat, raised up the basket with plantains, then took a few steps to the sink to wash her hands.

Julius Mosley and Maya Gaines were sitting across from each other by a window. They were unaware they were at Table 6, of course. Both had doubles, curried chickpeas inside fried bara, with plantains and cabbage on the side.

"You know the answer," said Mosley.

"But why? For real. Sifu, why do these exercises every day if not to use 'em in real life? If you go to a shooting range, it's so you can hit a real target when you need to, right?"

Mosley had a ready response. "Bruce Lee said it's better to be a warrior in a garden than a gardener in a war."

Maya wasn't fazed by this.

"Then you're saying we use our skills if a situation calls for it."

Mosley held with, "I'm saying we practice martial arts to learn patience and dedication to a craft. To build character. Confidence. Ideally a martial artist doesn't have to fight in the world. It's about peace. Where is this coming from, Maya?"

Chef Lisa stepped out of the kitchen and headed in their direction. Mosley and Maya noticed. He moved away from their topic of conversation.

"One of my favorite restaurants in town. Food you can't get anywhere else."

Chef came over to their table.

"How you doing? Like the doubles?" she asked.

Mosley started. "Great as always. Thanks so much."

"It's my first time here. Love it. I've never had anything like this," enthused Maya.

"Glad you made it in. Stop back soon." Chef Lisa smiled and headed over to the next table while Maya continued with Mosley.

"When I was coming home from work Sunday night, I saw some people about to get robbed. Or carjacked."

"Maya," responded Mosley quickly. He leaned forward.

"And I, I stopped it from happening."

"Are you okay?"

"I'm fine," she said. "It was easy. Just used some of the forms we practice. But I saw it happening in slow motion. Me handling it all. My body just moving automatically. Does that make sense?"

He took a deep breath. Her response calmed him, but New Orleans was a dangerous city.

"I'm glad you're alright. Yes, it makes sense. You're a natural. There's something in your soul. It's not just the physical movements. Anybody can learn those. But also the gift inside you. Most don't have it."

"Like a… warrior?" Maya was nervous to say it but hopeful for validation.

"That's a good way to put it."

"Then what's wrong with using that to help people?" she asked.

"Did he have a gun? The person you stopped," wondered Mosley.

"Um, there were two of them. They had guns."

"Maya!" Mosley collected himself. "You can't walk into that. You could've gotten shot."

"But I wasn't scared. It felt natural."

That didn't soothe his soul.

She kept going. "Maybe something's wrong with me. I didn't care they got knocked out. Kinda liked it too."

Mosley had to know. "Are they…?"

"I didn't kill 'em" she assured. "Just knocked 'em out. I used the spinning fists you taught us."

"You did?"

"They were the perfect distance apart for that. Sifu, remember you said Tong Bei is used for extended arms? But you think that's in me. The ability to kill?"

"No, no, no. I'm not saying that," he stressed. Mosley spoke slowly so no missed meaning.

"I wish you hadn't gotten involved," he continued. "But you did the right thing by helping people. Please be careful. This is why you wanted to talk? What was bothering you?"

Maya didn't show full expressions, only hints of this or that emotion. Mosley didn't know her, but he knew enough to tell the lightness in her voice was a ripple in the deep pool of anguish she was feeling. And it wasn't only about the altercation.

"I wonder if there's something bad inside me that likes hurting people. If I'm messed up."

Mosley got very serious. Didn't break eye contact.

"Maya, you're a brave person. Solid. You have a

sense of justice. The other day when those guys tried to come at the class? Remember? It took a minute, but then you were fearless. Not aggressive. Calm. Those are all positive traits."

She struggled. Should she tell him about her parents and why she thought she was destined to end up like them? Humiliated. Locked up. About Vinh Nguyen and why she met with him? Sifu Mosley would surely think of her differently if he really knew what she was like. What she'd do for money. About the hair pulling. The real Maya underneath it all.

"Thank you for hearing me out. I appreciate you meeting up. I can't make it to class today. Have an appointment," was all she could say.

"Okay. Let me read this to you," he said.

Mosley took *The Last Shadow* out of his gym bag and flipped to a page.

Before reading, he said, "This book changed my life. When I looked at myself and didn't like what I saw, the wisdom in here put me on the right path. A better path. I certainly don't know everything you're going through, but if you don't mind."

Maya nodded in agreement, appreciative too for the time taken. She had no doubt she mattered to Sifu Mosley, and not just because she was the best in the class.

"Change will happen," he read. "Trying to resist it is like resisting sunrise."

He closed the book.

"Maya, be the best change possible. Inside yourself."

"Okay. Thank you, Sifu. I really appreciate it. I'll be at class Wednesday."

"Let's see what happens with the hurricane. You used Tong Bei for real?" he asked.

"Yeah."

"Ice in your veins. Look at you."

"Really?"

"Yes, lil sister. Black Ice. That's who you are," he nodded, impressed.

Mosley stood up.

As they were walking across the restaurant for him to pay at the host stand, they passed Table 5 with three people. Maya didn't see the man whose back was to her, and he didn't see her either. Danh Trang was so engrossed in the conversation with the two across the table that he had tunnel vision. His hopes and dreams were in the folders they had between them and their glasses of sorrel, hibiscus tea

"Mr. Trang, you made it very easy for us," said Ernest Clark. "Didn't he?"

"Very much so," said Shelly Apuzzo to his right. "Strong background at well-respected restaurants."

"Especially Hangry. I'm never hangry when I leave there," laughed Clark.

Trang winced, but he stayed measured and respectful. Not a sign of annoyance showed on his face.

He'd heard this one before. Far worse too.

"Mr. Ernest, Hangiri is named for the rice barrel used to make sushi."

Clark took no offense. Threw up his hands and said, "See. Shelly, what did I tell you? Knows his stuff."

"Indeed," she agreed. "What else? Starting small is a good idea. Solid business plan. And a unique idea. Mr.

Tran, your application is exactly what we were looking for."

"Yes, sir. Take something already popular and turn it on its ear," chimed in Clark.

Trang made no assumptions. "This all sounds positive," he said.

Apuzzo beamed bright as the sun over the Causeway as she said, "It's more than positive. We'd like to offer you the full $20,000 small business start-up grant."

"To get your restaurant up and running," added Clark, but that was already clear.

The new restaurateur took a moment before speaking. First a sigh of relief. Next, thoughts of his parents, followed by a visualization of his bustling restaurant.

"Thank you, both. Thank you very much. This is great news."

"We appreciate you doing this in Metairie," said Apuzzo.

"Agreed. I've been on the Economic Development Commission for seven years, and your application is one of the best ones I've seen. You'll make Jefferson Parish proud," crowed Clark.

"If you can sign this to make it official."

She ceremoniously handed Danh Trang a document and a pen that he promptly used, as the restaurant's host brought their food orders.

23 IT MATTERS NOT WHERE YOU LAY YOUR HEAD.

Vinh Nguyen sat solo in his office. He took out a photo from a rarely opened desk drawer. It was from the time when people still had memories printed. There were two young people, both around the age of 20. Not a full year before it all happened.

He poured a glass of snake wine from the bottle on his desk into a shot glass. One hand held the photo. The other clutched his booze. Nguyen was drinking in a centuries-old tradition. Whole venomous snake infused in alcohol or rice wine. For health. Sexual potency. Plus, the alcohol had a kick.

Cuong did the same with little geckos that had been dehydrated, but it was snakes only for Nguyen. All privately done. Not public for non-Vietnamese or other Asians to see. Common in the home country, but the Anglos weren't ready for anything beyond pho and banh mi.

He got up and made sure both doors were locked.

As he sat back down, his view followed the curve of the snake that had been sitting for just over six months inside the bottle. That and the photo took him to Seward Park in New York City. July 1991. He and his sister Minh were walking parallel to Essex, just a little way from his shared apartment across the street. Edge of Chinatown.

They weren't deep in the park. That day they both

looked fairly similar as they did in the photo. The general traits. Eyes, nose, cheekbones, head shape, but there the familial similarities ended. He was cocky, flashy, and had a spiky hairstyle. Started going by Vinnie. She was proper, looked it, and dressed conservatively. Minh hated his new nickname too.

Nguyen remembered it well, because that afternoon walk haunted him more than anything in his life.

"It's not gonna happen," he'd said.

Minh had replied, "There are options. Choices."

"My other option is work in a restaurant."

"What's wrong with that? Me doing it will help pay for college. Why not you too?"

"That's not for me," scoffed Vinh. "I get respect this way."

"Respect or fear?" Minh fired back.

"Doesn't matter. The fuckity fuck shopkeepers don't talk down to me anymore. I don't care the reason."

"Your mouth. Such language."

"Such language," he mocked. "I don't care."

"You should. Very disrespectful. It reflects on me, your sister."

"Disrespectful to who? I have power with my friends."

"They aren't friends. It's a gang."

This conversation had played out several times before, but Minh persisted. Vinh was more adamant than ever before, though.

"Friends. Gang. What's the difference? Nobody messes with me. Nobody disrespects me anymore."

"They're just scared. They don't trust the police either."

Vinh sneered and puffed himself up, all 142 pounds worth, counting the clothes, shoes, and hair gel.

"You do it your way. I'll do mine. Vinnie way. Gonna be a big shot too."

Minh lashed out.

"You just do what the Chinese don't want to handle themselves."

"I'm an enforcer for them."

"You're proud of that?!"

"Why not? They made me part of their gang. How many Vietnamese you think the Chinese let in Ghost Dragons?" he said, not needing a response while he looked down at the initials tattooed on his wrist.

As Minh shook her head at him, they both turned to their left to see a NYPD squad car parking with squeaky brakes. The driver got out and ran toward them. The other one, in the passenger seat, also got out but promptly bent over like he was sick.

Vinh and Minh saw the police turn toward his partner. When he spun back toward them, he had a gun pointed. The drawn weapon bridged the last few steps.

"NYPD! Freeze! Stay where you are!" he ordered.

Minh was terrified. She spoke to Vinh. "We didn't do anything."

"I told you I didn't want to take a walk. Shit! Don't speak. Not a word," he told her.

They were commanded to, "Turn around! Hands behind you!"

As Vinh turned, he saw the police check back. He was a *mi trang*, white person. The other policeman still doubled over dry heaving was a *mi dang*, Black person.

If only Vinh could call out to his guys, his brothers, his fellow Ghost Dragons half a block away and four floors up. They'd come out and blast these foreign devils. Maybe they saw it happening from the window.

But no one came.

No one else but Minh heard the police mock him with "Pssssh" and a look of contempt.

No one else but him heard the police say to Minh, "Let me start with you. Make sure no weapons," before he patted her down in areas only a lover would know.

No one saw hands linger there but him, or heard his sister be spoken to with, "Ooh baby. We gotta continue this later. Getting me real hard."

No one else saw her horror. They weren't coming. Vinh stepped toward the police, shoved him away from Minh, and pulled out his own gun as the police fell to the ground, his service weapon still in hand.

Vinh saw in his peripheral the other police now running toward them. That meant another gun.

"Drop it!" yelled the one on the ground.

Minh did a Minh type thing. Why this time? She darted over to shield Vinh but also to keep him from firing. To keep him clean. They weren't twins. She was a hair older. Never failed to remind him of it or act like it. But why now?

At her sudden movement, the police on the ground fired. Vinh heard Minh cry out and saw her fall. As she crumpled, he had an unobstructed view of the man who killed her. The police had a flash of realization at his mistake, and he paused. Vinh blasted without hesitation. Eye for an eye. Life for a life. It was Minh, so two lives in exchange.

Vinh turned and fired at the oncoming police yelling, "Freeze!" who would've been casualty #3 if not for proceeding wobbly. The man still went down, though, dropping his gun and holding his shoulder. Vinh looked at his sister. He wanted to stay by her side. Hold her. Bloody or not. Or should he make the next shot count with the squirming police on the ground? His split-second decision was to flee and not be captured by the other cops bound to come.

Vinh heard over and over behind him, "10-13! Officer down! Officer down!" And Minh was back there all alone.

That night hadn't ended before Vinh stepped onto a bus leaving Manhattan. Only a duffel bag to his name. No one else with him. Ghost Dragons told him where to go, but he was on his own.

It wasn't yet afternoon two days later when he woke up in New Orleans.

There was no doubt a different life was beginning when his feet were submerged in water while he worked the rice fields out by the swamps of New Orleans. Like he was a peasant. A farmer. But a Ghost Dragon remains a Ghost Dragon. Even though he got word that most of them were rounded up to be locked up. Was he the last one left?

Vinh remembered the first time one of the other field workers stepped to him. His sorrow for Minh held his arms down and shrunk his spirit. Saving face didn't matter, but not the second time. He'd made the man pay. Felt good too.

He sighed and poured another shot before tears

slipped down his cheeks.

24 THE SPIRIT IS CAUTIOUS.

MAYA SAT ACROSS FROM HER AUNT NEKISHA FISHER WHO WAS taking a rare lunch break at home. Meaning barely more than five minutes sitting at the table and bookending it while eating and driving to and from work. This was important, so be it.

"Baby, I appreciate you. But no."

"You're sure?" asked Maya.

Aunt Nekisha had been initially leaning forward to hear out what Maya had to say. Now she settled back in her seat. This wasn't up for debate.

"Without a doubt," she said. "Money solves most problems. But this, I couldn't live with myself."

"Okay. I'm relieved."

The older woman stood up and walked behind her niece's chair to wrap arms around her. A softer voice from deep within said, "You have a gift. No doubt. But they aren't gonna put their grime on you. I'll make due."

"I'll let him know. Gotta give that money back," said Maya.

"Every dollar," stressed Aunt Nekisha. "Be careful, though. Let him save face. Male ego. Want me to go with? Would have to be after work."

"I got it."

"Alright."

Maya had worry remaining in her soul. "Thank you," she said. "It's not me at all. Doing that. I just thought…"

Her Aunt squeezed tighter.

"I know your mama and daddy, God bless 'em, have their problems. Your soul is genuine and filled with goodness. Now I gotta get back to work. Let me know once it's been handled."

She paused, studied Maya, and added, "Girl, your mama's wig. You wear it well."

With that, she left, and Maya took out her phone.

"Maya?" wondered Julius Mosley.

"Sifu. Mr. Julius. I wasn't completely honest with you. Didn't tell you everything."

"What's going on?"

Since she'd just gone over it with her aunt, Maya spoke of the situation in a similar way.

"At the gas station. When I, I stopped the guys trying to rob those people, somebody saw me."

Mosley was wondering where this was going.

"Maya?" he asked again.

"A man wanted to hire me. He said bodyguard, but I think he wants me to hurt people."

"Oh no."

"I'm sorry," she said. "I didn't know at first that's what it was. There was a lot of money. It kinda blinded me."

"I get it. I'm not judging you. What are you gonna do?"

"I'm telling him no. I didn't realize."

Mosley felt relief.

"Glad to hear that. I really am. Maya?"

"Yes."

"Who is this person? It's not just the money. What

you know about him? Do you want me to get him to lay off you? I used to be on the police force back in the day."

"I think once I give him the money it'll be alright. You were a police officer?"

"Sure was. Who is this person?"

"He's a businessman, but I think he does shady stuff too," said Maya.

"Sounds like it."

Maya continued. "His name is Vinh Nguyen."

This startled Mosley. A name he hadn't heard in decades. It couldn't be.

"Say that again."

"Vinh Nguyen," she said slowly. "Maybe I'm pronouncing it wrong."

"How old is he?"

"Um, I don't know. Definitely older than me, but maybe younger than you."

Mosley kept probing.

"And from his name is he…?"

"I think Vietnamese," she said. "His office is in the Vietnamese community anyway. Out in the East."

"Maya, one last question. Did you notice a tattoo on his right wrist or hand. Letters 'GD'."

"I don't know for sure, but I did see part of a letter on his wrist. Maybe a 'D.' Do you know who he is?"

"I might," he said. "Alright, be careful, okay. Call me if anything."

"I will," she said, and they hung up.

Julius Mosley was in shock.

Maya said to herself, "You got this. I'm glad I talked to him. Be strong, Maya. What does Sifu always say?

Deep breathing."

Tongue to the roof of the mouth. Breathing long in and out through the nose. Belly expanding on the long breath in. Receding on the long breath out.

Mosley was in his home office. He took a shoe box out of the closet and removed his NYPD badge from it.

"25,211. Those were days," he recalled as it all came rushing back.

New York City was plenty wild then. He was wild too. Early 1990s back when anything could happen, and it often did. Mosley and partner Tony Greene were Officers in the 7th. One of the smallest precincts in Manhattan, but that didn't matter. Plenty going down. They didn't patrol the Alphabet City streets. Junkieville, they called it. The 9th had to work those. Plenty of drug biz on his side of Houston also. Tenements, squatters, burned out buildings. The smell of trash. Artists and creative people too.

The Giuliani days would come a few years after he left that little slice of crazy. Mosley hadn't been back, but there was plenty in the news about how New York had changed. He wondered if it still felt at all like how he remembered it. A mish mosh of immigrant groups. Jewish, Puerto Rican, African, Cuban, and an extension of Chinatown.

The Feds were on the warpath back then. Going after gangs in 1991. Name a group. The Feds were trying to nail them. Big focus on organized crime. Even the household names of the Italian Mafia and the Chinese Tongs right across from Little Italy. Officers Mosley and Greene had been briefed on what was coming next for them.

Was it to help bring down the Gambino or Lucchese

families? No, there was a list with photos of the kids who did the dirty work for the Chinese. High stakes. Low money. Guard the gambling houses. Shake down the merchants. Run the drugs. Put a bullet in whoever had it coming. Mostly Vietnamese young men with nothing to lose.

Mosley and Greene were only a few blocks from the precinct house. Just driving. No striving. They both must have been barely pushing 30, if that, back then. Heading north on Rutgers before it became Essex when it kicked around the park. A route they'd been on hundreds of times.

"My head 's killing me," said Mosley.

Tony Greene laughed a knowing laugh. Hair of the dog. It was nice to get a break from Moto talking so much.

"Lemme know if you're gonna puke," he said.

"Yeah."

"The usual?"

"Shots. Too many," groaned Mosley. "Tia's gonna give me a shot to the head I keep coming home like that."

"It's just drinking."

"Black women don't play. I may have passed out in the bathroom," said Mosley.

At that Greene laughed showing teeth. Theirs was a salt & pepper partnership in NYPD, meaning a rare interracial duo. They got along fine, though the rest of the precinct thought it was fishy.

"Moto, you end up with toothpaste all over you again?"

"Not this time. Appreciate you driving."

"Got you partner," said Greene.

People were out and about. It was New York City.

Walk a few blocks. Pass by 100s of others. Some spots were a little more sparse. Like Seward Park to their right.

"Tony, slow down. I think he's on the list," said Mosley, looking in the park.

Green was skeptical at any powers of deduction coming from his cadaverous looking partner, especially to surmise that one of the couple they saw was pertinent to them.

"How can you tell? They all look alike."

I remember him from the photos." Mosley persisted. "His hair. He's on the list. Ghost Dragons."

"Big crackdown isn't for another week." He looked at Mosley in disbelief. "In this condition, you want to start taking your job seriously? C'mon, Moto."

"But he's here right now. None of his guys around. Doesn't look like much. Maybe not even armed."

Greene was driving. It would have been easy enough to put his foot back on the gas pedal, but he noticed something else.

"She looks good," he said. With that he pulled the squad car to the curb. Both of them cursed. Brakes so squeaky gave them away every time. Greene got out and immediately began running.

Mosley tried to do the same, but he had to immediately double over once he stepped out. He could feel whatever was left in his gut about to come up. Saw Greene look back at him before his partner removed his weapon from his holster while continuing to run.

"NYPD! Freeze! Stay where you are!" Mosley heard him say.

He saw the young Vietnamese couple talking to each

other. Neither fleeing. Maybe he was wrong, but the guy looked like a gang member he'd seen during the training with the Feds.

"Shit, nothing's coming up," he muttered to himself. Felt like a knife to his insides. The wave of nausea rolled up and down his body. He had little presence of mind. Enough that he heard his partner say, "Turn around! Hands behind you!" Might have even seen his partner quickly look back at him again, but he didn't hear what was said after that. Didn't see his partner grope the young woman for kicks.

Mosley forced himself to stand up straight and briskly walk toward the scene. That turned into full on running, as best he could, gun drawn, when he saw his partner shoved to the ground. Greene yelled "Freeze!" as he and the young man pointed guns at each other. The guy was armed after all.

"Shit! Shit! Shit!" echoed in Mosley's mind.

Before he could get there, the young woman jumped in front of the man.

"Oh no, Tony," thought Mosley as his partner fired from the ground and killed the young woman. In response, the young man, the one he had said they should pick up, shot and put a hole in Officer Tony Greene that Mosley thought would never close.

He ran up from the side close enough to see the distinctive "GD" wrist tattoo. He was right. Ghost Dragons member.

"Freeze!" Mosley called out.

Over the years, he had kicked himself more times than he could remember that he didn't fire before the one who killed his partner spun and put him on the ground too. The one who put that bullet so strong into his shoulder he couldn't keep his weapon from falling out of his hand. The one he expected to put another bullet in him to finish his life but instead looked down at the young woman lifeless in front of him before running away. The one that a few hours later Mosley learned more about.

"10-13! Officer down! Officer down!" was all he could do. He'd failed his partner and himself. No denying that. He soon found out the girl was an innocent civilian. The sister.

There were three memories that remained from the aftermath. First, sitting in his little apartment and drinking while Tia left him for good. On the table in front of him was a splashy New York Times story about Ghost Dragons gang member Vinh Nguyen shooting and killing NYPD Officer Tony Greene. Barely a mention that Minh Nguyen was also shot and killed.

Once Mosley was good and plastered, he drove back to the same area, staggering around and accosting every young Asian man he saw. Making them show their wrists. Treating them roughly, as if they were the one who'd killed his partner.

Second was Julius Mosley receiving a Medal of Honor from the shootings. NYPD brass knew it was as fake as he did, merely a PR stunt to play ball with the Feds and help them spin the imminent crackdown on organized crime, though Mosley himself was pulled off anything to do with it. His toxicology report was doctored. He said all the right things.

In return Mosley was to receive a guaranteed pension,

but he stayed on the force for a few years, merely to try and undo his mistake, and get street justice for his partner. Nobody wanted to partner with him after what had happened to Greene, though. They openly called him out by his name. Mean mugged him in the precinct and on the streets. The racist stuff got worse than usual. He felt so low he let it slide, and it got worse.

Third was Mosley holding open a big trash bag and throwing away his liquor bottles after pouring all the contents down the drain. That didn't stop him from being an irritable dry drunk seeking vengeance for Tony Greene. He came across various Ghost Dragon members before the Feds did, but no one would talk about Vinh Nguyen. He eventually left for New Orleans. The Medal of Honor didn't come with him, but the pension did.

All the memories. The past was now back in the present. Nguyen was a common last name, but his instinct told him this must be the same Vinh Nguyen. In the same city. Over 1,300 miles away from where it all went down. Acting the same. Criminals, like most civilians, rarely change.

Mosley put his NYPD badge down. He was at a loss for what to do next. The man with all the answers had none.

25 GREAT TIMING IS UNTIMELY.

Vinh Nguyen was seated at his desk. Photo with his sister tucked away in the drawer. Jimmy had gotten his nose manipulated to realign it after Nguyen's lashing out. Nothing major, though. Set and bandaged for now. He stood, as usual, and kept his distance.

"Can I trust this Kiri Tree? Of course, Cuong can be trusted. He's been with me for years. Drank the blood of the Ghost Dragons," said Nguyen.

"*Đại ca*, boss. I did too."

"Right, right. If Kiri Tree gave us Bao Vu's girlfriend and his own *mi dang*, Black, boss, it's for me personally to dispose of the rat faced fuckity fuck. Taking over the 7th ward almost makes me wish Bao Vu would be alive to see it. Calling me a farmer!"

He spat into his trash can.

The buzzer from up front crackled over the speaker and had Nguyen looking to his desk at the security camera he used to monitor the jewelry store up front.

He saw Maya Gaines. Unexpected.

Nguyen gestured for Jimmy to open the door and signal her to come back. The employee up front standing by the buzzer was confused by this but certainly wasn't going to question the boss. Maya entered the office with her right hand in her pocket. Left pocket held 10 bands. She stood situated between both men. This wasn't a time for sitting. She eyeballed the room, particularly the bottle of snake wine on Nguyen's desk.

"My dear, you're a day early. But very well," said Nguyen, turning on his Vinh charm.

"Thank you, Mr. Vinh for receiving me," she said.

"It's fine, Maya. I assume you came to handle the problem you saw in the other building."

"I really appreciate you seeing me. My strength. My power to have your back."

Maya made sure to get all the upfront politesse out of the way.

"Of course," replied Nguyen.

Forging forward, Maya said, "But I don't think it's the best for me. No disrespect."

"Hmm. You think it's beneath you." Nguyen didn't miss a beat. If he was surprised, he didn't show it.

"Oh, no, no," she said.

Nguyen's eyes tightened. He'd kept her from seeing Vinnie so far, but it was time. "You're forgetting two things. You took the money. You saw the woman being held. There is no choice. You already said yes. I own you. Same as him," he gestured toward Jimmy.

"Mr Vinh, I'm returning the money. I can't do all this."

He was amused. Sniffed the air around him intentionally loud and long.

"Did you know when we smell something unappealing to us, it's already too late? We've already breathed in the molecules of whatever the stench is. Useless fucking bitch. You stink of lies and cowardly behavior. You think you can just leave here? Can you already smell what's about to happen to you?"

Maya shuddered, paused, and right back at him, she said, "My phone's in my pocket. I have a text ready to send saying that you have a woman held captive. My finger's been right above the send button the whole time. I'm gonna give you this money, walk out the room, and delete the text once I leave."

Jimmy inched closer. Maya saw it and expected the move.

"You got me. Such wisdom," said Nguyen. Sarcasm dripping. Smiling with malice. "Give me the phone. I'll send it myself. Guess what, you fuckity fuck? There's no one in that building anymore. My plans changed. She's been moved, so send your text."

This was unexpected for Maya, but she kept her resolve and spoke as a distraction.

"I told you I can't do this. But it…"

She threw the money at Nguyen who ducked and reached into a desk drawer for his gun. Maya then sunk low, spun, and did a leg sweep to put Jimmy flat on his back. She was kind enough to leave his nose alone but used the blade of both hands to firmly strike the nerves below both ears. Had him stunned and his equilibrium would be off kilter for long enough. Next, she flipped the lights off.

The room was lit only by the faint glow of the security camera. A couple quick gunshots, commotion, followed by stillness. The jewelry store employees and customers were still running outside in fear when Nguyen's office door opened. Maya stepped through it and walked confidently through the store and outside, past the cowering people.

A joyous man was driving home, saw the scene, and

pulled into the parking lot. He lowered his window.

"Maya?!"

She was a bit confused, not knowing who she could trust. He looked familiar, though.

"Who are…"

"It's Danh," he reassured. "Danh Trang. I used to work at Brassy."

"Yes, yes."

"Need a lift? What's going on?" he asked.

"Please, yes," she said. "I'll tell you on the way.

Maya got into the car, and Trang sped back the direction he'd come from.

26 OUR ORIGINAL NATURE IS OUR ORIGINAL NATURE.

WEATHERCASTER JULIE CORMIER HAD THE RAPT ATTENTION OF many on Wednesday morning. She summed up the hurricane status before Mayor Rosalind Elloie, Police Chief Clement Denny, Director of Homeland Security Howard Fullerton, and others either provided updates and necessary information or stood in solidarity.

Mayor Elloie and Chief Denny may as well as had their titles prefaced by "The Beleaguered." She had turned her critical position into a part time job with full time partying. He seemed hapless to handle the worst murder rate in decades. Both were grateful for an emergency situation in which they were no longer the subject of continuing questions and headlines.

"Hurricane Izzy is expected to make landfall overnight. Weather conditions will deteriorate beforehand. Entergy notified customers in the New Orleans area to expect a loss of power for up to seven days bare minimum. All but one of the Sewerage & Water Board pumps were working. No mandatory evacuation, so no contraflow on the highways with all lanes going away from the city. The Governor Freddie Pool had requested federal disaster relief funds for expected needs. Senior citizens or those with special needs were requested to call 311 for shelter transportation. Those in lower lying parishes closer to the Gulf of Mexico were told to expect storm surge. Everyone should make sure to be stocked up on supplies of water, batteries, canned food, toilet paper, and more."

As the live press conference continued, there were thousands of stories playing out in New Orleans. One was taking place at the swampy edge of the city inside a disused World War II-era ammo bunker in the woods. Both Quincy 'Q' Adams and Cai, Bao Vu's girlfriend, were bound, gagged, tied back-to-back together, and seated on a large tree branch that resembled a long stump. For good measure, their movement was restrained by a rope that tethered them to a thick branch.

Danh Trang and his mother Lan were in a long line at the grocery store a few miles away with a cart full of water, canned food, and snacks.

Sister Pat stood outside her 7th ward restaurant to watch the sky and smoke two cigarettes. In that time she saw Flora Mosley leave from upstairs. She suspected why the young woman was there. Drugs, of course.

She puffed away and pretended not to see Bao Vu and Teo show up and head through the same iron door. But even though she didn't know that they came to confront Tree why there'd been no contact or response from Q, she knew to call Vinh Nguyen and tip him off when she stepped back inside. She wasn't the only one paying attention from the street.

Samira and A.J. Mosley brought plants inside, secured objects, and finished preparing outside their Riverbend home for the hurricane.

At Brassy in the French Quarter, Maya Gaines was working in the kitchen. As usual, she wasn't in the mood for what Elvin had to say.

Vinh Nguyen was throwing Maya's returned money at Jimmy and Cuong. He no sooner had gotten off the phone with Sister Pat when Tree called. Both of them thought Nguyen sounded extremely stuffed up but didn't speak on it. This was for the best, considering his nose was bandaged like Jimmy's, and the bottle of wine lay broken on his wet desk with snake sprawled out courtesy of Maya.

Julius Mosley was sitting in his car at the parking lot for Nguyen's jewelry store and the other shops. He looked at the location on his phone. Widened the city map and saw he was way out there. Almost the last residential area before the marshes and Lake Pontchartrain led to the North Shore. He scanned across the other direction, seeing City Park, before his eyes led to the Mosley family home on Leonidas, steps from the levee and a handful of batture houses on stilts. The last few standing that were built between the Mississippi River and the levee.

He shifted his gaze back to the right. He was sitting and waiting at the second address he'd been to. Armed with a printout from the Orleans Parish assessor's website listing all the buildings shown to be owned by Vinh Nguyen. Hadn't seen the guy in 30 years. Couldn't find any photos online. Would he even recognize Nguyen or vice versa?

Next to the address list was Mosley's copy of *The Last Shadow*. It was open to the following entry: "Our original nature is our original nature." He flipped to another page.

27 BE MINDFUL OF MORTALITY. SPEND TIME WITH NATURE, WHICH HAS BEEN BEFORE AND WILL BE AFTER US. TREES FALL. WHO ARE WE TO THINK WE WON'T?

SAMIRA MOSLEY PACED AROUND THE HOUSE HOLDING HER phone up like a beacon she somehow expected to beckon help. Wind gusts were picking up. Thunderstorms getting heavier. Hurricane on its way. But her husband wasn't there. A.J. and Flora sat at the dinner table.

"Pick up. Pick up. Why are you not?" Samira scolded the phone.

"You're sure he doesn't have a class?" wondered A.J. "In this weather?"

A.J. shrugged. "It's the kind of thing he would do. I remember when I was a kid. We were walking Canal Street. Dad made me stop for a minute and close my eyes. Told me to use my ears and nose. Imagination too. To get a different experience."

"Daddy likes a challenge," agreed Flora. "But I wish he was here."

Samira sighed and looked directly at each of them in turn before speaking.

"You two aren't making me feel any better. I told you he cancelled martial arts class in City Park today. Regardless, it's not like him. No response for hours? During the hurricane?"

"Maybe you should report a missing person," suggested Flora.

"Sometimes I wonder about you," shot A.J., who pursed his lips and shook his head at his sister.

She'd heard and seen it all before from him.

"Judgmental. 'Cause I care about Daddy."

"Ohhhh, that's what it is."

"A.J. Not now," said Samira.

"Just because I think he's okay. Dad can handle anything."

"I'm sure you're right. Still wish he…"

Samira tailed off as the front door opened. A soaked and dripping Julius Mosley stepped inside. They all rushed to the door. He was unfazed by it all.

"Where have you been?" asked Samira. "Why didn't you respond?"

"I had to handle something. It's funny how things turn out."

"What'd I tell you?" said A.J. to his mother and sister.

Mosley said, "Ran into an old friend. In a manner of speaking."

A.J. lifted his arms, palms up.

"I rest my case," he said.

"Sorry, was in the forest. Left my phone in the car."

Samira wasn't satisfied with this. Not at all.

"With a storm moving in?! You were surrounded by trees. Not a great idea," she said.

Julius Mosley kept his casual composure and responded, "Turns out it was the best move."

"Daddy, what's that mean?" asked Flora.

Mosley took his copy of *The Last Shadow* from a

bag and held it in front of him so he wouldn't drip on the pages.

"This says it all," he said, flipping to a particular entry.

"Be mindful of mortality. Spend time with nature, which has been before and will be after us. Trees fall. Who are we to think we won't?"

Samira was exasperated with him. "Meaning?"

"I've been in the woods. A.J., grab me a couple towels," he said.

A.J. gave his mother an "I told you so" tilt of the head.

28 WHAT IS IN YOU WILL BUILD OR BURY YOU.

Hurricane Izzy didn't need to be a direct hit to impact New Orleans. A power grid several decades old. An antiquated pumping system run on that same power grid and by a computer system that looked like it was from a mid-century black-and-white movie. Power outages and street flooding were simply what happened in the city. A solid two hours before the hurricane moved through, most all of both sides of the river had no juice. Heavy rain continued to move through in cycles.

Maya and her Aunt Nekisha played chess by candlelight, as per tradition. Despite best efforts by the older woman, Maya was winning. Same as always. Aunt Nekisha had no knights, a few pawns, and a scattered number of pieces left.

"You're always two steps ahead. Mind so sharp. Probably all those books you read."

"The more you play, the better you'll get," Maya encouraged. "Don't give up those knights so quick next time. Crucial pieces, but you treated 'em like pawns."

"I see that now. And I see you doing the right thing by giving that man his money back."

"I couldn't do what he wanted."

With that Maya picked up her phone and checked an app.

"Nor did I want you to," stressed Aunt Nekisha.

"Everything straight?" All handled?"

When she didn't get a response, "Maya, phone."

"Sorry, Auntie Kish. Needed to check on something."

Maya had barely put her phone down before she moved her bishop and announced, "Checkmate. It was handled, but he wasn't going to let me leave, so I had to fight my way out."

"Child…"

"I know. He didn't leave me a choice."

Aunt Nekisha lowered her head while she lifted her eyes upward.

"Alright," she said. "We'll be leaving this place soon enough anyway. New part of town. Things have to get better. My soul needs it."

Yes, Auntie Kish. I know it's harder for you because of me."

"Don't you even think that. Don't say it either."

Maya said, "Okay. I'm trying. I really am. Everything you've done for me, I appreciate it so much. But when I look at myself. Compared to anybody else, I mean. It's Daddy and Mommy I compare myself too. I know I'm good at martial arts. It's a gift. But is it a curse too? Mommy's so good with numbers. Everybody says it. You do too. Can do calculations in her head. A whiz at math. And Daddy. He's the people person. Told me, 'Maya when I leave a room, there are no strangers to me anymore.' He meant it. The two of them together, a power couple. $1 + 1 = 5$. But now they're locked up far away. I can't help… okay… I'm gonna say it. I can't help but wonder if what brought them down was because of their strengths. You know what I mean? If they got to a point they thought they could get away with anything, 'cause Daddy could just talk away the problems and Mommy make the numbers dance. What if the same thing is in me? Martial arts is my blessing, but what if it's what brings me down? That's what I wonder before I go to bed. Am I blessed or cursed?"

29 FOLD INTO FAMILY.

The Mosley's had their own hurricane tradition. Julius, Samira, and A.J. were sipping wine and talking by flashlight. A.J. had his question-of-the-day calendar out to spark conversation. Since they didn't consistently do it, the family had chosen to start with the question from a few days past.

"Here's a good one. What was your happiest school moment as a child?" asked A.J.

"That's easy for me," said Samira. "The praise my 2nd grade teacher gave me for the story I wrote about kangaroos."

"Kangaroos?" A.J. was astonished.

"They were my favorite animals. Jumping around with the baby, the joey, in their pouch."

"There you go. Good memory," praised Mosley.

Samira continued, "They're very interesting creatures. Tail as long as the limbs. Can hop around 25 feet forward but can't go backwards."

"That's got me beat. Now I know why you've always wanted to visit Australia."

"Yup, there you go. Simple as that," Samira replied to her husband. Next to A.J. "Where's Flora?"

"She, uh, wanted to be by herself."

"What are you not telling us?" asked Mosley.

"I think you should talk to her about it," A.J. responded.

At that, Julius Mosley rose from the table and left the room to have a word with his daughter.

30 NO PERSON CAN LEAD ANOTHER.

Vinh Nguyen was drinking in the Antoinette Hotel bar as if there were no hurricane. Jimmy and Cuong were by his side. Electricity was on, and the air was blasting. The crime boss was on the phone.

"Power grid is underground here. For what I'd pay for a generator, may as well just stay in a fucking hotel a few nights. Plus, high ground just in case the levees can't handle it."

The caller was saying the kind of thing that made Nguyen swell with pride.

"Exactly," Nguyen responded. "If it turns into a mess for the community, we rebuild same as we always have. So why you calling?"

This time the caller raised Nguyen's ire.

"Really? That useless little asshole?"

Jimmy and Cuong were groaning inside, wondering if one of them was being spoken of. They were only lightly soothed when Nguyen announced to them, "Danh Trang was seen driving away with the *mi dang*, Black girl, after she left."

Nguyen returned to the call. "Thank you, my friend. I'll return the favor."

He couldn't jab at the button hard enough to hang up.

"History repeats itself," he said to the two men seated around the table. "I made his big mouth fuckity fuck father zip his lip. Now it's Danh Trang's turn."

Nguyen stared down Jimmy.

"This is your chance to redeem yourself. First, I get Bao Vu after the storm passes."

31 FIND SOLACE IN SILENCE.

OTHER THAN THE FRENCH QUARTER, ONLY A FEW FLUKE HOMES
and buildings had working electricity. Street lights were
out. Tree limbs were down, making a handful of streets
impassable. The quiet of a power outage isn't realized
until it happens. For the morning to come, cars wouldn't
be able to gas up. No grocery stores would be opening.

32 B FOLLOWS A REGARDLESS.

THE MORNING AFTER HURRICANE IZZY WAS TIME TO TAKE inventory. Julius and Samira Mosley were picking up things outside. Their own and those of neighbors that had blown into their yard. They set lawn furniture upright. Talked as they tidied up.

"Looks like a few shingles blew off. I'll need to get someone on the roof," said Mosley.

"If I hear roads are clear, I'll send A.J. down to the Quarters to get ice for the fridge. Don't want to lose everything."

Like the seasoned hurricane veteran she was, Samira had put all the freezer and refrigerator items into garbage bags before Izzy came through. If power didn't come on quickly enough, it would be much easier to throw them out. Plus, in the event of a sudden evacuation, they'd be able to return, toss the bags in the trash, and not lose the fridge over it. Hurricane Katrina had taught many that stinky lesson.

"Right, good call," agreed Mosley. "Better him than…"

"Flora." Samira finished the sentence with what they both knew.

"She sees a good time and thinks I don't want her to have any fun. She doesn't know what I know."

"We can't coop her up the rest of her life. Hopefully she reins it in."

Julius Mosley sighed. "She's heading back to school before too long. All we can do is trust her."

"I know."

"We had a good heart to heart. Felt like a breakthrough anyway. Is she telling me everything? No. Did she tell me more than before? Absolutely."

Samira was waiting for this moment. The events of the previous night had been weighing on her. Julius showing up soggy after being unavailable to reach for hours.

"Baby, speaking of, tell me more about yesterday. Do I need to be concerned? It's not like you."

"I know, my love. You have to trust me. Just know it all comes down to karma and kinetic energy. Can't have an outcome until there's motion. Make sense?"

"Cause and effect," she said.

"Action and consequence," he added.

"The kind of thing people don't believe exists anymore." Mosley was firm. "But it does. And in this particular situation, it will."

"Julius?"

"That's all I can say. Not trying to be mysterious. It's better this way. Sometimes it's best that you let somebody get what's coming to them."

"Okay," Samira didn't push.

"I will tell you this."

"What's that?"

"I learned I'm a kangaroo." He raised his eyebrows at her.

"We got a fool here."

"Seriously. Yesterday taught me big time about not moving backwards. Not being that person even when it's calling so strongly to pull you back."

"Good. Out there hopping in the rain with your jokes," she teased, but her glance was wary too.

"I'm hopping over here to clean this up."

Mosley walked over to a cluster of downed tree branches. He picked them up, paused, and remembered.

33 OUR ORIGINAL NATURE WILL GAIN DAILY FAVOR.

WHILE JULIUS MOSLEY STOOD IN HIS YARD, HE COULD SEE THE memory of yesterday as if it kept happening in front of him. Sitting in his car, meditating in a parking lot. Taking in the pain and grief of others along with a long breath in. Joy and peace from him to them with the outward air. All through nostrils. Eyes open. Watching. Waiting. Putting himself in the situation to come. Not knowing exactly how he would respond. Would this change his life? How it went down in New York decades ago sure did.

He ran through possible scenarios again and spoke aloud to himself. "Just to see Vinh Nguyen. Look at him after all this time. No more? Can I just leave it at that? I dunno. And who knows what his response will be. This man killed my partner. Do I still want vengeance? There are two ways this'll go down. Either eyeballing Nguyen or I'm taking him out. For good reason. Not only for killing my NYPD partner. Trying to turn my student Maya into a Ghost Dragon killer. Death or jail her only outcomes. Vinh Nguyen is a poison on this earth."

Mosley sighed and squinted at the jewelry store front door, reading the letters "*Tốt Nhất* Jewelry Store" in red above it before he continued. "Flora's my daughter. My flesh and blood. My baby girl. I love her dearly. Would never tell anyone, but Maya's more like the daughter I wish Flora was. Has her head on straight. A whiz at martial arts. Maybe Flora will get there some day. But, man, look. Vinh Nguyen, it's coming down to you and me after all these years. That's it."

Mosley did another round of meditating. Was Nguyen even there at the jewelry store? Mosley looked at his address list. Yes, this had to be the spot.

Next, Mosley read from *The Last Shadow*. He knew the entry by heart at this point, but seeing the words was important to imprint upon him. Over almost two hours it'd been sitting there propped open. "Our original nature is our original nature," Mosley said. He repeated it. Slower this time. He flipped to another entry and did the same with it.

Light rain began along with wind gusts. He puzzled at how one book entry might be ambiguous and the other precise exactly at the time he needed to have certainty. No grey area. These words were putting the onus on him. Was his original nature the young drunk motormouth who ruined things? His first marriage. His NYPD partner. Nguyen's sister. Himself. Or was his original nature what was underneath all of that messiness? What was left once he began the scary process and construction project of clearing the debris to excavate his soul?

Samira kept calling and texting. He couldn't answer or respond. It stung him to put fear in her, but this was something he had to do solo. He needed to stay in the zone. No distractions. This was a major life decision. The minute Maya told him about Vinh Nguyen, he knew this would happen. He wasn't Julius Mosley, son, husband, father, ex-cop, martial arts teacher. None of that.

He was a creature ready for battle if that's what it

came to. Mosley was embracing one of two pillars—either the purity of the soul or the purity of violence. The former sounds great, but what would happen to Maya? The latter comes with a price. Once you kill, you have to keep killing. It gets messy. Payback comes calling. And the stain stays on the soul. Was it worth sacrificing himself for Maya's sake? On the other hand, how could he possibly peep the man, size him up, and then proceed on as if unseeing Nguyen?

34 DO NOT LET EVIL ENTER.

Most of the outside security lights hadn't worked in years, and evening had come. Back in the day, over two dozen businesses had flourished on both floors of the long building, but now it was down to seven. Six if Nguyen didn't get rent paid on time from Mr. Le at the grocery store. Julius Mosley had little doubt who was about to exit when the jewelry store's front door opened. The employees had already left and flipped the closed sign, but there was one car still in the parking lot other than his own. A nice one too. He was parked next to it.

The man in the middle of the three walking out had the same eyes, the same expression Mosley remembered from decades prior, even with the nose bandage. He looked like he hadn't been missing any meals. No longer young, but still resembling the younger version. Mosley had to be certain, though. No doubts. Not for what might happen next. What the true original nature would do.

Mosley didn't have much time. He got out of his car. Didn't rush. Relaxed. Methodical. Deliberate. He saw the two men next to Nguyen immediately on guard. Even more so the closer he came. Hands reached in for guns. Didn't matter what they had if he was going to handle them. Odd that one of the two also had a bandaged nose.

The birds and other outdoors animals had done their squawking and chattering earlier in the day. They knew a storm was coming. But now they were hunkered down.

Except for a lone crow who flew overhead Mosley, Nguyen, Jimmy, and Cuong, dipping to no further than three feet above their heads, before rising back up. As it did, it cawed and jawed five staccato sounds before a long drawl. Its cadence took Mosley back to age eleven in church and Pastor Himes repeating "Give the dev'l no place," a phrase he'd never forgotten. As the bird soared out of eyesight, Mosley repeated the phrase in his mind.

He made sure his forward motion toward the three appeared neutral. Knew, being ex-NYPD, what few do. Battery is the act of harming a person, but assault is the fear of being imminently harmed. He didn't want to allow Nguyen any justification, instinct or legal, to have him shot. Mosely continued closer. He sized up how he would take them all out. Use their close proximity to each other. First, handle the gunman closest to him. Second, get Vinh Nguyen tangled up with the second gunman. Third, take down this other guy. That left Nguyen to be dealt with 1-on-1.

Here was the moment. Everything slowed. Their movements. His movements. The wind gusts. Thoughts. Past. Present. All of it shifted from a tiny dot to a large circle where Mosley had all the time in the world in a span of a moment. The metronome of a clock ticking then stretching and droning on into an eternal second. He realized this must have been how Maya felt when she took down the two young gunmen she told him about. She hadn't explained it this way, but he wouldn't have fully understood it then anyway. How do you get your head around eras of existence compressed into one slight snap of the fingers?

Mosley was about to reach the point of impact with the men. Was it time for vengeance? He made conscious effort not to prepare his fists. He saw himself as a child, an old man, with a bird head, with Nguyen's head, and no head. Saw Nguyen and his bodyguards as babies, 200 years old, and looking like a composite of everyone Mosley had known over his life and those he was yet to meet.

Once they were as close as they had been since the horrifying day in New York City, Vinh Nguyen's physicality shifted as bodies flew in from around him and clumped onto him. Each of them had a frozen grotesque look on their face. A death mask. Mosley could himself feel the sheer weight of Nguyen add up quickly as each body merged with his. It slowed the crime boss. Mosley saw Nguyen's future was to aimlessly walk the earth with poundage so strong from his own actions he could barely lift his knees. Almost forcing him to crawl. Shuffling along an endless knot of his own making. Simultaneously, Mosley was filled with a surety about Maya and Nguyen that flooded his mind with a stunning sudden knowledge.

The answer was clear. The answer was easy. Mosley's original nature was indeed his original nature. "Be patient," he said to himself. It all made sense, and the speed of time and space snapped back in place. He nodded to them as he continued past. Jimmy and Cuong swiveled around to make sure an attack wasn't coming from behind. They wondered, who was this strange man? He didn't look like he lived in the area. He didn't belong, but he was moving along.

Nguyen's two henchmen took their hands out into the

open again. Nguyen himself remembered nothing from the past. Mosley held no distinction for him. Just another weird fuckity fuck Black guy outside with a hurricane on the way. Probably another junkie. The three men got into Nguyen's car.

Mosley smiled broadly. "Give the dev'l no place." His life was beginning right now. This day. This time. He nodded to himself as he walked a bit further. Saw small homes with chain link fences almost as tall as their roof lines. Apartment buildings on the other side of the street looking like they were one step from collapsing. He turned back to his car to see Nguyen was gone.

He spoke to himself with only the sky as his witness, "Maya will be covered, and Nguyen won't have control over her. I don't know how, but I'm certain. Know it as solid as I know my name. He won't escape the consequences. It's coming soon for him. His suffering will be continuous."

35 A WALK IN THE WOODS IS MEDICINE.

By the time Mosley drove the short distance to Bayou Sauvage woods, rain was coming down much harder. He had no umbrella. Didn't want one. Wouldn't help much anyway. He hadn't been to this nature preserve in years, much less part of town, but needed to come down from the heady moment with Nguyen. The forest would do the trick, the entry from *The Last Shadow* guiding him there. Once he got back to the car, he'd reach out to Samira.

It was no surprise the parking lot was empty. Who else would possibly think it was the perfect time to hike there with an impending hurricane? Julius Mosley was wired differently. Despite the thunderstorms and stronger gusts coming through, this was about purification of his soul. He was in no hurry. Walked along the path and sat on a stump for a minute. Listening to the rain rushing through the trees. His clothes soaked and clinging to him like a second skin.

Mosley felt compelled to step off the official path. Why? For some reason it seemed like the right way, or maybe he heard something. He wasn't sure, but he moved forth through the trees. Mud threatening to slurp up his shoes. When Mosley was to the point where it was time to turn around or he might not find his way back to the main path, he had a surprise. The downpour couldn't keep him from seeing a unique building the overgrowth mostly hid.

It was as tall as a single-story house, but there the

similarity ended. It looked like an old above-ground bunker as if it were half of a massive pipe that had risen from the forest floor. He couldn't tell how far back it extended, only that only that it was made of concrete and had a metal door for entry.

He opened it and was as shocked as those inside. Lighting was limited to what the sky provided, but he could make out two people. They looked to be captives seated back-to-back on a large tree branch. They were tied to each other and the tree itself. Water was sloshing up to their ankles. He could tell they were both terrified. They looked like they expected to die that very evening.

Mosley first removed their gags.

"Are you okay? How long you been here?" he asked.

"Get me outta here," said the Black man who Mosley guessed to be in his mid-30s.

"I need to let Bao Vu know I'm okay," said the young Asian woman. Mosley put her barely into her 20s.

At this, the man still tied to her turned his head in surprise.

"Bao Vu? You the female he's looking for?"

"Yes, yes."

The man didn't let this news get in the way of his irritation at Mosley's pace at freeing him.

"I told you, get me loose."

Mosley stepped it up. Tight knots and wet hands made it tricky.

"Vinh Nguyen did this. Very bad man," the woman said.

Mosley was blown away.

"You said Vinh Nguyen?"

She nodded vigorously in agreement.

"Who's that?" wondered her fellow captive.

"You know Bao Vu?" she asked.

"Yeah," he said wincing at the pain of Mosley tugging ropes loose.

"No, I don't," said Mosley.

"That's my man," she said. "Mr. Vinnie, he kidnapped me to get back at Bao Vu."

Q, now rubbing his sore arms and stretching his shoulders, was angry.

"Then that muthafucka got me too. Been working with Bao Vu. But how Vinnie know where…?"

He looked over to see that the woman was also freed. Now he was in charge. "Let's bounce," he commanded.

"Rain's coming down hard, but I'll get you home," said Mosley. "We have plenty to talk about on the way.

The three of them headed to leave the bunker and the onslaught of rain and wind.

With this, Julius Mosley finally opened hooded eyes to see that he had returned to his backyard where he was picking up debris from last night's hurricane. Samira was watching him with concern, not hearing him mutter, "Consequences coming, Vinh Nguyen."

36 IF B DOESN'T FOLLOW A, CONSIDER IT A BLESSING.

BY THE AFTERNOON OF THE FIRST DAY WITHOUT ELECTRICITY, the heat was kicking. New Orleanians were sweaty and salty. Kiri Price, known as Tree, was in that number. He sat on the couch in black jeans. No shirt. When he needed to cool off, he'd take a shower.

Tree was feeling pretty good about himself, though. Flora's friend Brittany showed up unexpectedly. He'd popped off at her before when the two of them came by shortly after Vinh's guy Cuong did a number on him. Working with them now. Feeling fine being the top dog with Q out of the way.

Brittany made her way into Tree's place with more than the hint of a twist in her walk. He hadn't missed it either.

"Them gas pumps might be off 'til next week. You needed to drive over here real bad," he said.

"Maybe I did," said Brittany, who stood facing him. "Gonna call me bitches again?" she asked as both an accusation and an aphrodisiac.

"Nah, we straight. Without your lil friend, huh?"

Eyebrows raised. She knew what he meant.

"Glad I don't have to check you again. I figured we could work something out. She can pay for her shit," Brittany said.

Tree waited to see what she meant, but it didn't take

long. She slipped off her top. Unbuttoned her jean shorts. After sliding them down her hips, they easily dropped to the floor. Red lace panties and bra accentuated honey caramel skin.

"Body tight fa sho," he said.

Brittany walked over to hm. She knew this would work, because it always worked. Why not?, she thought. Take advantage of it while she could.

"I knew you wanted me," she said while scanning his body with her eyes.

He tried to act coy. "What you talking…?"

Tree couldn't finish his sentence. The door was kicked in. His soul sunk. Brittany let out a shout and grabbed a blanket to cover up. Tree didn't bother to budge. Let his piece stay under the couch, only because by the time he could react he saw Quincy "Q" Adams, who was supposed to be dead, and two Asians in the doorway. Not the ones Tree was working with either.

All three of them had Glocks pointed at him. He knew Q's Glock 18, the military grade automatic pistol. Wartime and law enforcement weapon. Nothing to play with at 1,200 rounds a minute. The two men he'd never seen before were holding brown Glocks. Tree knew these were 19s. Probably with switches on the back, to turn a semi-automatic gun into a one touch fully automatic fire. Like a small machine gun.

This is what he grasped in an instant along with knowing it all was bad for him. Best to leave his hammer in its spot for the time being. Reach under, grab it, and shoot all three when the moment presented itself. For now, try to work it out.

"Q, it ain't like that," he said as he stood up and stretched to his full 6'5". This had been his automatic way to assert, show presence, and intimidate since his growth spurt at age fifteen. Coach fell over himself recruiting Tree to play high school basketball, guaranteeing college scholarships and big dollars. Young Kiri Price had no time for long practices and short promises. He only cared about two things back then. Regular visits to either Tyra Hill or Mikayla Pittman's places when their parents weren't home, and a weekly barbershop visit to keep his hair clean and tight. Didn't want it to brush against the top of doorways. He quickly developed a hunch and forward lean along with a scowl and quick fists for anyone who mocked him.

"Sit your ass down," announced Q. "You know why I'm here, bro. I was buildin' business. All you had to do was come along for the ride. Do your thing. Get paid. You fucked up, Tree."

"Q! We brothers."

"Shut up! Look at you. Bitch ass. Yeah, we got history. That's on me. Didn't see it comin'. You knew at the barbershop them men waitin' outside to throw me in a trunk. That's why you stayed inside and took a leak, right? No confusion who to grab. Tryna play me?!"

"Nah, nah. They lying."

"You a lie. With your foul shit. It's a lie I got left to die with this man's woman in a hurricane?! Muthafucka, I was there!"

Q pointed at Bao Vu, who took it as a sign to step forward. He had bad intentions for Tree and was jumping out of his skin to avenge his queen's abduction.

Q put his arm out to stop Bao Vu. "This mine," he said. Q didn't mind Bao Vu's show of force for intimidation-sake, though.

"Say the man's name behind this," Bao Vu demanded.

"I ain't saying shit to you," scoffed Tree.

"Then say it to me… brother," Q added with a calm flow. "Or I chop off your dick and feed it to you. Got caught up in the paper chase. Gotta pay, playboy. No more good hair pussy for you."

Brittany normally would've popped off in return, but not this time. Instead she instinctively touched the end of her hair.

Kiri winced. "Maaan, look. Shit."

Q remained matter of fact. The man he faced was dead to him. This payback was to remind the streets who ran the 7th.

"You gonna die. You gotta die. Go down like a soulja, Tree."

Those were the words to make it work. The key to unlock the puzzle. Kiri wasn't afraid to die. Expected it for the past 28 years, ever since age six. Saw those who looked like him were born to die. Wouldn't be around too long. Gonna die. Gotta die. He had a longer run than most. Knew this was it for him. They weren't letting him leave the room. Tree looked over at Brittany. Had it been ten minutes later, he could've had that good pussy too. Knew better than to ask for that as a last request, though.

"Fuck!" He took a few moments. "Alright. Mr. Vinnie," he admitted to Q.

Tree added to Bao Vu, "Mr. Vinnie hates your ass." Dropped his eyes. Knew what was coming. Don't start none if you don't want there to be none.

Q nodded. All the history, the years he'd been knowing Tree, that was over. The only concession to it was that Tree wasn't going to get tortured.

"There we go. I checked. Got word you had some visitors. Streets talkin' 'bout you takin' over my business on the slick. I see what you up to. But… you kept it G. Fessed up. For that, I'mma do you better than you did me."

Q turned to Brittany. "Say, beautiful. All this ain't you. So we straight, normally I don't want a female to see this. But this time different."

Tree drew as much air as he could into his system and looked at his shoes.

With no hesitation, Q pumped a couple rounds into the lowered head of Kiri "Tree" Price. The supplicant pose, as if in prayer, quickly became a grotesque display of carnage. Brittany was terrified she'd be next. Especially since the one they one called Q was staring directly back at her.

"You here to fuck the dealer," he said to her as a statement, because there was no question.

She was in no position to respond coherently.

"I was just… please… I won't talk," Brittany managed to get out.

Q put his gun in his waist, walked over to her, took her purse, and removed the wallet. He wasn't looking for money. Instead, he peered at her driver's license.

"Brittany Casimir. Stays on Prytania Street," he said aloud to himself.

Q flipped through her credit cards, insurance card,

and such until he came to a family photo. It was from a recent photo shoot at City Park with Brittany, her little brother, and her parents.

"Ohhh, shit. Who-ee," he exclaimed. "Your daddy Jim Casimir on the city council."

He looked at Bao Vu.

"My man, ain't never gonna have a problem again getting that shipment in from Houston."

Bao Vu didn't know what was meant by this, but he couldn't miss that Brittany was shaking with terror.

Q pointed at Tree's body. "You wanna die like him?"

"No, no."

"Alright then, Miss Razzle Dazzle. You gonna road trip to Houston once, maybe twice a week."

He said, "She do anything we need," to Bao Vu, who was skeptical. He had his own people.

Q put most everything back into Brittany's purse and handed it to her.

"You work for me and B.V. Got a problem with that?"

"No. No problem."

He held up the Casimir family photo and her driver's license with one hand and placed his other one on her shoulder. "Because if you do, Daddy, Mommy, even lil man here get hit. Or Mr. Jim Casimir gets set up with some drugs and hoes."

She could barely emphasize, "I'll do it."

Q squeezed her shoulder hard enough to get the towel draped around her in his fingernails and said matter of fact, "Best believe you will. Easy peasy road trip and keep your mouth shut."

He wasn't worried about her doing anything other

than exactly what she was told. He'd had other party girls work for him before. His only concern was making sure she didn't partake in the product or claim theft to sell it herself. Be a surprise if it didn't happen. But Q could handle bitches. He was sure to tell anyone so. He had put the last disloyal one, Tree, in the grave without thinking twice.

Q turned to Bao Vu.

"I handled my shit. Now it's your turn. Get the man who put this in motion. Dead his ass."

Bao Vu nodded with murderous thoughts of Vinh Nguyen.

37 IMPATIENCE LEADS TO A GREAT FALL.

THE LOBBY OF THE ANTOINETTE HOTEL WAS PACKED BUT NOT nearly as much as the bar. Plenty of locals had come down to the French Quarter to feel normal and bask in the magical a/c. Staff was spread thin but no one more than the bartender, Nathan James. Typically, a Thursday night presented no problems for handling things solo, but not the day after a hurricane. Big tip night, though, and being extra busy still beat sitting in his shorts inside a hot house.

Vinh Nguyen knew he wouldn't be waiting for his next drink. Tipping strong the previous night had paved the way for his sway. He was feeling himself too.

"Tonight it starts. Four bullets. If you both can't handle it with just four, you're fucking useless. They won't have more men than that that. Not discreet."

Jimmy and Cuong knew that a packed place with many witnesses wouldn't necessarily keep the boss from doing to them in public the same thing as in private, so they fixed their faces and responded with a polite "Yes, *đại ca*, boss."

Nguyen continued, "Then tomorrow, you get rid of disloyal Maya and Danh Trang who helped her. I want those two gone by…"

He checked his watch.

"11:02 p.m. Twenty-four hours. I just need one bullet tonight for my shot."

"Bao Vu," said Cuong.

Nguyen was mortally offended merely hearing the name.

"That skinny rat face. Ghost Dragons won't stand for it. Sister Pat is *cục vàng*, piece of gold. How else would we know what went on at the apartment above her restaurant? They killed Tree, our new business partner. It helps that those shitty people have loud mouths she could hear from the first floor."

He praised Cuong.

"Good work on leaking our location. How did you let Bao Vu's so-called queen and his new friend Quincy got away though? You fucked up again."

"I know a man with a big mouth," said Cuong. "Guaranteed he'd run to Bao Vu with it. We had the two of them tied securely. Same as we've always done. Someone must have come upon them, but Bao Vu is extra mad now."

Jimmy nodded in agreement.

"No doubt they will come tonight. Let's go get ready for them," said Nguyen.

He rose, and though Jimmy and Cuong hadn't finished their own drinks, they joined him and brought their cut crystal glasses with them. The group zigzagged through the crowds who at that point had made the hotel lobby a makeshift overflow bar and social mixer area. As usual, once confirming their elevator was clear, the two men stood in the front to prevent anyone else from stepping in once Nguyen had entered. They grunted "Full" a few times to merrymakers who wanted to wander upstairs and to hotel guests who had the bad luck of picking hurricane season for a vacation.

The locals weren't too bothered since they could simply take the next elevator to check if a random floor had an unlocked room where they could crash for the night. The tourists, on the other hand, took the hurricane as a personal affront. Treating their good time like birthday balloons that snuck up to the ceiling and hovered just out of reach before deflating and taking a humbling nosedive to the floor.

Nguyen's timing was on point. No sooner did the three men close the door to their room on the 6th floor, then Bao Vu, his sidekick Teo, and Quincy "Q" Adams entered the hotel. All of them focused and furious. Itching for revenge. Sporting big hats and sunglasses to cover up for the hotel cameras. Bao Vu winked knowingly at the woman standing behind her Concierge post, as she had provided him earlier with the necessary information in exchange for enough money to make it worth her while. He had sworn to her that nothing would happen under the roof of the hotel. Not a drop of blood spilled. Not a bruise inflicted.

That was a promise he didn't intend to keep. Vinnie Nguyen and anyone with him were gonna get hit. What could the concierge do about it anyway? She was complicit after all. Room numbers were valuable information, and she coughed up Nguyen's for barely a pair of tickets to see a Saenger Theatre musical.

Teo put his right hand in his pants pocket. Not for a gun or a weapon. Only to have his fingers on what the concierge had slipped to him outside, away from the hotel cameras. With his left, he tapped the elevator button for "6."

When the men were steps from Nguyen's room, they got their guns ready. Teo took out the key card for room 612, transferred it to his left hand, and got his Glock ready. They all silently looked at each other. Bao Vu pointed to Teo, and the key card was inserted. The minute they saw the green light and heard the corresponding click, Teo opened the door. He and the other two rushing behind him quickly found a dark room. They led with their weapons, took a few steps, and all toppled like buffoons in an old silent film. After falling flat, they didn't get back up. Not a gunshot was heard.

After a few seconds ticked, a muffled voice yelled in the hallway.

"Call 911! Call 911!"

38 IF OUR LAST SHADOW CAST IS AS THE FIRST, THEN WE HAVE THE WAY. MOUNTAINS ARE NOT RIVERS. FORESTS ARE NOT DESERTS.

JULIUS MOSLEY AND HIS STUDENTS WERE ENJOYING THEIR Friday afternoon. Much better to be outdoors and feel a little breeze moving through the woods than to be inside stuffy homes. Electricity wasn't due back on for at least three days according to the news.

"Tomorrow we'll focus on standing meditation. Zhan Zhuang," he said.

Sifu Mosley was facing the six, including Maya. At least being in City Park felt like some kind of post-hurricane normalcy. No flooding to speak of. Only some downed tree branches in spots, pruning the old oaks.

He and the students bowed to each other the usual way. The way they both began a class and closed it out. Open left hand at an angle meeting right hand fist at chest height. Slight bend at the waist. There were various explanations of what was meant by the Kung Fu or Shaolin salute, but whatever the reason, it had been a mainstay in China for 1,000s of years.

As they were finishing, a car pulled into the parking lot with the radio turned up loudly enough for them to hear, "Breaking News--New Orleans is reeling from both the aftermath of Hurricane Izzy and the arrest of six men at a Canal Street hotel Thursday night. According to NOPD, the men had homemade bombs, chemical weapons, and illegal firearms. There is no word yet where they planned to use them, but authorities are extra watchful of the French Quarter. Please use all caution and report any unusual activity. Stay tuned for further updates."

Maya Gaines walked with two of her fellow students to the parking lot.

"Did you hear that? Bombs and chemical weapons," said the person Maya called Headband in her mind, because he wore what seemed like a different decorative one every practice. She also knew that when sparring he was vulnerable on his left side and didn't like to deliver or receive kicks.

Red replied, "It's crazy. Glad they caught 'em. A lotta people coulda been hurt." Red was called that by everyone based on his bushy beard. It was a unique look what with his shaved head. He was a high school wrestling champ and still loved to fight on the ground. With him, Maya knew to make him work on his feet to protect his face, which would then open up a soft midsection that beer had built over the years.

"Yeah, scary," replied Maya.

"I wonder if they were going to blow up the hotel?" asked Headband.

This wasn't a question expecting an answer. Headband and Red said goodbye and kept walking when Maya stopped where Mosley was standing. He looked at her quizzically.

"I saw an interesting name in the news this morning. The thing they were just talking about on the radio," he said. "Vinh Nguyen sounds like he was wrapped up in a lot of terrible stuff. Bombs. Poison gas of some kind."

"I didn't even know about all that. He never talked about it in front of me."

Mosley studied her. "I'm glad for your sake he'll be locked up for a long time. For everyone's sake. It's an odd way for him to go down after all these years. I guess it was bound to happen, though."

"All these years?" she questioned.

"I assume he's been involved in this for a while. It seems strange too all of them named or in cahoots."

"Why is that?"

Mosely responded. "Terrorism didn't really seem like their thing, and you know how it is. We typically don't mess with Vietnamese people like that and vice versa. They do their thing. We do ours."

"Think about all the other things he hasn't gotten caught for," Maya said. "Things he probably did."

"Right, right," agreed Mosley. He was wondering more but didn't ask. His star student was trying to get out from under the thumb of a crime boss who wanted her to hurt people. Probably kill. And then he goes down. About to get thrown under the jail for the first time. Mosley had known sure as anything that Vinh Nguyen would not be able to escape the consequences of his actions. That's why he hadn't taken Nguyen's life in front of the jewelry store, but, yet, there was something more to this.

Their talk was interrupted by a sudden sound. A stunning heron of three colors with dark wings and light underside announced itself as it flew overhead. They followed it across the sky with their eyes. Maya had a quick flash of four memories. It was as if a sudden waking dream came to her. Not an eternity in a shot glass or several lifetimes in a second the way that Mosley had experienced it the day before, but in the blink of an eye the four brief memories coursed through her. All bound by one number, 612.

First, Maya was standing in Vinh Nguyen's office shortly after telling him she wanted no part of his organization. He and Jimmy were on the floor briefly unconscious. Maya thought for a moment before turning on the lights, putting down a piece of the bottle she'd swung at Mr. Vinh, taking the crime boss' phone from his desk as snake wine from the now-broken bottle and the snake itself spilled out across it, and installing a tracking app. She saw a text from the Antoinette Hotel confirming a reservation for Room 612 starting the following day, Wednesday. Maya then flipped the lights back off and left.

Next, Maya was in Danh Trang's car while he was driving her to safety. Once they arrived at Aunt Nekisha's place, she thanked him, sat on the porch, and took out her phone. After searching two different word clusters online, "what crime longest prison sentence" and "animal tranquilizer gas," then reading about them, she took a walk along Mandeville. First time stopping at what was known as the "Million Dollar Corner" because of all the drugs sold there. The hustlers and the zombies looked at her suspiciously, but they were quick to come around, glad to bring someone else to their level. Or so they thought.

Once she found that Scar was the drug dealer who had the TNT, the good stuff, that grey death, not milder tranq, they walked together on Derbigny until midway down the block. She followed the lanky man along the walkway between the Caribbean-blue shotgun house and the squat converted body shop next door all the way to the back of the long house. Once inside, she confirmed that Scar truly had pure Carfentanil, 100 times stronger than fetty.

The anesthetic for larger animals was exactly what she was looking for, and not to cut it into heroin or cocaine. Not to take down elephants. After her purchase of two white flakes and a couple homemade devices that Scar's roommate specialized in, she hid them in her room and headed up Elysian Fields to the big home improvement store for aerosol cans and more.

Maya's subconscious continued to work rapidly. Taking her inside Aunt Nekisha's when the hurricane rolled through the following night. Electricity was out, and they were playing chess by candlelight. Aunt Nekisha said, "Nor did I want you to. Everything straight? All handled? Maya, phone." Maya had picked up her phone to check tracking of Vinh Nguyen and saw he was in a hotel on Canal Street. Had to be in room 612.

Still, she knew her aunt's rule about being present. "Sorry, Aunt Nekisha," she said and put her phone down. She moved her knight into place and called out, "Checkmate." Her Aunt had a look of astonishment while Maya answered the question. "It was handled, but he wasn't going to let me leave, so I had to fight my way out."

Lastly, just before Maya was beginning to open her mouth to speak to Sifu Julius Mosley, the folds of her cerebellum were the tracks of a Japanese bullet train as it picked up the pace even more so. The chronology took her to the previous night. This time she was walking steadily through those massed in the Antoinette Hotel lobby while wearing the biggest wig her mother had. She didn't rush but neither did she dawdle.

Hood was up. Backpack on. Motion steady. In her peripheral, she saw Mr. Vinh, Jimmy, and Cuong drinking in the hotel bar. This registered nothing upon her face, even the bandage upon Nguyen's nose. No recognition. No anger. No delight. None of it shown. She had a job to do, and she moved through the lobby, choosing the 6th floor when the elevator doors opened.

Maya took the first "Do Not Disturb" sign she saw hanging from a doorknob. Now she wouldn't need the old credit card she brought. Upon reaching room 612, she put on gloves, worked the plastic sign in the space between the door and the frame, and flipped the latch. As expected, no one was inside. She quickly closed the door and confirmed with the tracking app that Nguyen wasn't on the move.

Maya put the backpack down and removed a baggie and two homemade bombs. Neither explosive device would be set to detonate. That wasn't the point of it all. Both were placed in the bathroom on the sink. Baggie on the nightstand. Next, she reached into the backpack to take out safety gear that she used to fully cover her head. Two aerosol cans came out of the large backpack. One was placed on a nightstand, and she held the other. Then she waited. Standing, not sitting. Watching her phone.

Eventually she saw from the tracking app that Nguyen was on the go, which she assumed meant coming her way. Where else would he go? Time for action. She sprayed vigorously from the can she'd prepared, focusing on the area nearest the door. Maya continued to spray until the aerosol can was completely empty. She flipped off the lights and stepped back. Little time passed before Nguyen, Jimmy, and Cuong entered the room. As she had hoped, they were overcome by the gas and fell to the floor. Maya knew her next step. She flipped the lights on and quickly headed to the bathroom to retrieve the bombs. After using the three men's hands to press firm fingerprints on them, she placed them both on the bed.

Maya took Vinh Nguyen's phone from his pocket, deleted the tracking app, and called room service. She didn't speak and left the phone off the hook, putting it on top of the baggie with one flake of the Carfentanil. She didn't want to kill them, only put them in a compromising position. The phone went into Mr. Vinh's hand. Maya was planning to leave and have that be the full of it, but she heard a rustling at the door. She no sooner turned off the light and hid behind the door before the familiar click resonated throughout the room.

She could make out three more men entering the room. Even in the shadows, she could still tell from the hallway light that they each had guns extended in front of them. The next day in the news, she heard that their names were Quincy Adams, Bao Vu, and Teo Hoang. Like the prior trio, they also quickly fell to the floor. Maya flipped the light back on one last time and sprayed a bit more from the second aerosol can before placing it in Mr. Vinh's empty hand.

For her final steps, Maya closed her backpack and left, calling out, "Call 911! Call 911!" even though it was muffled by her headgear. Took the back way out of the hotel to the alley. When she found a good discreet spot just before Iberville, she removed her gloves and headgear, put them in a plastic bag, and discarded it. Pulled up her hood, and that was a wrap.

As the final of the four memories zipped and dipped through her conscious and subconscious, Maya said, "They should be locked up a while for what they did. Remember the question I asked you?"

"Why train to be a ninja if you never use it in real life?" asked Mosley, while wondering if she was about to admit something to him.

Maya took a copy of *The Last Shadow* from her bag and flipped to a page. It was her own copy of the book, and she didn't search randomly. Mosley was pleased.

"Hey, hey," he said.

"You talk about it so much, I figured I should read it. This one is cool."

Mosley may not have shown it on his face, but he beamed inside as Maya read, "If our last shadow cast is as the first, then we have the way. Mountains are not rivers. Forests are not deserts."

"Yes." He knew that entry well.

"This sounds like we should try to be our true selves, whoever we are," she said.

"Exactly," he agreed. "Only don't try. Just let it be. Let it come."

"I'm figuring that out. Black Ice, though. That's what you said, right? What you think of me?"

Mosley laughed.

"Yes, that's what I said. It's cold facts. Don't you go and get a big head. Won't be able to get through the door."

“Could never happen.”
They both knew she was right.
“Alright,” said Mosley.

39 RESTORE BALANCE BY ACTING WITHOUT ACTION.

ABOUT THE AUTHOR

Michael Allen Zell is a New Orleans-based novelist, journalist, screenwriter, and playwright. He is best known for his crime fiction series featuring Bobby Delery, a Tulane University Criminology professor, who is forced to right wrongs on the streets of New Orleans.

Michaelallenzell.com
Instagram.com/michaelallenzell